ALL SWEPT UNDER THE RUG

ALL SWEPT UNDER THE RUG

BEVERLY MCCOY (HARLOW)

XULON PRESS

Xulon Press
2301 Lucien Way #415
Maitland, FL 32751
407.339.4217
www.xulonpress.com

© 2017 by Beverly McCoy (Harlow)

All rights reserved solely by the author. The author guarantees all contents are original and do not infringe upon the legal rights of any other person or work. No part of this book may be reproduced in any form without the permission of the author. The views expressed in this book are not necessarily those of the publisher.

Printed in the United States of America.

ISBN-13: 9781545620892

INTRODUCTION

*S*hould we ever sweep anything under the rug? This is a story about a young girl that spends much of her life sweeping her burden under the rug. Her burden is revealed but swept back under the rug. It stays under the rug for a while and then erupts again and again. This takes place in Southern California during World War 11 and the rest of the 40's

Preface

*P*lease Jesus, don't tell my Mother, I will never play that game again.

The purpose in telling Peggy's story is considering some of the thoughts and devastation a young child endures after her accusation of sexual mistreatment. Peggy is seven years old when she looses a close relationship with her mother. Her Mother finds it more tolerable to put on blinders than to acknowledge that her daughter is in harms way. Peggy has also lost trust from her aunts and uncles because there is no physical evidence that she is being sexually abused. However, she is continually being sexually insulted and annoyed during this period of her life.

It is my opinion that young children do not make up stories about being sexually abused. How could they have such sexual knowledge that a penis gets big and hard?

The story of Peggy takes place during the Great Depression and World War 11. This story is also a picture of Southern California during that time.

THE MAIN CHARACTERS

Margret Grabs, Peggy
Julian Dorsey, Peggy's mother
James Grabs, Julian's first husband, Peggy's Father
Sarah Jean Grabs, Peggy's sister
Richard Dean Grabs, Peggy's brother
Theodore Tucker, Julian's second husband, Peggy's stepfather
Ralph Tucker, Theodore's father, Peggy's step grandfather
Theodore Glenn Tucker, Peggy's brother, Peggy's joy
Grandma– Anne Tucker, Peggy's step-grandmother
Bobby, Larry, Jimmy, Peggy's step-cousins
Ray, Ida May. Maryanne, Peggy's step-uncle, aunt & cousin

Irene, Peggy's step-aunt, she is the Mother to Bobby, Larry, Jimmy and Jane

The Dorsey's, Peggy's biological family

Harry & Ruth Dorsey, Peggy's grandparents

Archibald Bell. Peggy's, step grandfather Ruth's second marriage.

Caroline Dorsey (Bernie Summers, Ralph Tucker, Gordon Mottley) Peggy's aunts & uncles she was married three times.

Caroline's Children, Peggy's cousins: Howe, Henry, Herb, & Marylou

Virginia Dorsey (Paul Key's) Peggy's aunt & uncle

Pauline Key's, Peggy's cousin

Sadie Dorsey (Merle McCall) Peggy's aunt & uncle

Brian McCall, Peggy's cousin

The Dorsey Brothers, Peggy's uncles, Allen, John & Fred

The Monkey's, Peggy's cousins to include herself, Howe, Henry, Herb, Marylou, and Peggy

Dale Fadner, Peggy's good friend

Fred Fadner, Dale's father

Lillian Anderson, Peggy's good friend that lives in the hills, close to the Fadner's

Mr. & Mrs. Wilson, Peggy's school friend's parents

Susan Wilson, Peggy's new school friend, with a limp

Sally Wilson, Susan's sister who is blind

Ann, Peggy's best friend forever.

CHAPTER ONE

Once I was a little girl just so high Ma, Ma, took a switch and made me cry. But now I am a big girl and Ma, Ma can't do it so the world took a thorny switch and hopped right to it

"Arkie!" the tall, skinny boy yelled from across the pollywog pond. I just starred, not knowing what an "Arkie" was. He threw some pebbles at me and I took flight.

I wasn't supposed to be there anyway. It was my secret place. With tadpoles, frogs and horny toads to play with, I knew that one of those pollywogs were going to turn into a frog or maybe a toad and I wanted to see it happen.

I left plenty of time not to be late for school. I never saw this boy before not all summer. I never saw any Kids here. Of course there were a few bent and rusted cans and some dirty old candy paper on the ground but not much. It didn't look as though anyone had been around for a long time.

The loose sole of my shoe flopping around caused me to stumble, throwing me in to a patch of long wild grass. The tall boy caught me, held me down, and yelled, "Arkie, you come here again and I will throw you into that pond!" He let me up and took off running toward the school.

Now it was time for school to start. I could almost hear the first of the two bells ring. The first bell was a warning; the second bell, you were late.

My Mother will whip me with a sapless peach or Apricot switch because I knew Miss Dotson will send a note home with me and tell her I was late.

ALL SWEPT UNDER THE RUG

I had to find a string or a rubber band to hold my shoe together so I could run. I was not allowed to take my shoes off because Mom said I would get hookworm from the ground and die.

There was an old rubber band on the ground, but it broke, I found some string by the pond and tied it around my shoe. I ran all the way to school. *"I am not scared of that boy,"* I thought. I'll beat his (Ass-k-me-no-questions I'll tell you no lie) if I see him again.

I walked in with green grass stains on my new school dress, the hem sagging, and my sleeve half torn off. *Snicker, snicker* came from my 3rd. grade classroom. One kid stretched his lips with his thumbs, stuck his tongue out, and wiggled his eight fingers at me.

I had known them, for only three days, and they were already making fun and laughing at me. I didn't think anything was funny, and I will prove it to them at recess.

They'll not think it's so funny when I give them Indian burns and twist their arm up behind their back until they say, "Uncle Sam". (Indian burns were a common expression used in cowboy and Indian movies and games during the 40's.) They probably don't even know who Uncle Sam is.

They don't even know how to have air-raid drills or how to play Germans & Japs or Army. They haven't even learned how to dip their pen in the ink well yet or write instead of print.

"Margaret", the teacher addressed me sternly, using my name. What happened to you? My name is really Peggy; everyone at home calls me Peggy. At my other school I get to write, "Peggy" on my arithmetic and spelling paper.

Your name is Margaret Grabs. The class exploded with laughter. "What happened to you?" "Nothing" I muttered in a low voice. *"I think I am going to cry*, I WON'T, *and I am going to throw away the note",* I thought. *When Mom sees my dress I am going to get whipped anyway.*

The odor of cesspools penetrated the atmosphere in the hills where I now lived. Just eight miles East of Los Angeles from where my family came. Los Angeles had it's own smell too. Mostly like foods and old cooking oil.

In 1942, the war was hot, and at my school in Los Angeles, we had air-raid drills everyday. The warning bell would ring, and we jumped out of our seat and squatted at the side of our chair. Mouth open, hands over our ears, with our head tilted to the floor and we stayed in that position until the "All-Clear" bell rang.

When the sun went down, it was blackout. Lights out, windows and doors covered with whatever to keep in any light, even the flickering of a cigarette or a flashlight. Every night the "Patrol Wardens" canvased the neighborhood for offenders.

Los Angeles in the forties was a smelly, dirty old place with sex perverts, alcoholics, and tramps (what we call homeless people) roaming the city that somehow managed their way through the Great Depression of the mid thirties.

No matter, Julian Dorsey, my mother, said that she would rather live in the gutters of Los Angeles than to go back east where she came from, and nothing could ever make her move from Southern California. California seemed warm to her even when others said it was cold. To her, it was comfortable even when the temperature raised over one hundred degrees. Compared to North Dakota it was her paradise.

Today Los Angeles in the twenty-first century, is a smelly, dirty old place with sex perverts, drug addicts, homeless, illegal immigrants, and food stamps. The topography has changed, gangs have different names, and technology has given to most the gift of a smart phone. The closet doors have swung wide open for all to see the city's shameful evil behavior on display.

During World War 11, Los Angeles was a major center for wartime manufacturing, shipbuilding, and aircraft building. It was the headquarters of six of the countries major aircraft manufactures (Douglas, Hughes, Lockheed, and more), which brought growth to Los Angeles County.

Before the war, Los Angeles County was a forest of orange groves. The fragrance of orange blossoms was intoxicating, sweet, and wonderful, and there wasn't a tract home in sight, not in that area, anyway. A short distance out of the Metropolitan Los Angeles area brought you into million upon millions of oranges. There were lemon groves and olive groves. The mountains were on one side, the ocean on the other.

Unfortunately Los Angeles has a fog season, a smog season and approximately 10,000 earthquakes a year, though most of them are too small to feel. However, a few made global headlines.

The Los Angeles County Hospital and University of Southern California Medical Center is an icon to Los Angeles, noted for charity. The hospital was established in 1885. Today it is one of the largest public hospital and medical training centers in the United States. The 1994 Northridge earthquake changed the safety codes, and the hospital did not pass. They built a new hospital that consists of a diagnostic and treatment clinic, an inpatient tower with 600 patient beds. They still take care of the unemployed and poor.

Today Los Angeles and Los Angeles County has the second most population in the nation. People are still flocking to it. If you can't get it there you don't need it.

For most people that I have meant, the city or state that they grow up in influences our diet, language, accents, ideas, and beliefs that make an impact on our lives. I have heard Los Angeles compared to a salad bowl, meaning that every culture and Nationality in the world have made their home there. This is my home and I am proud to have been part of it.

My story is just a portion, an eighth of my life, living in the country and the city of Southern California with a tremendous burden that influenced my life.

CHAPTER TWO

First school days, what a joy, I loved the girls. I loved the boys. I liked my teacher, but she didn't like me because I talked too much and made a fuss and ruled her bunch.

The cutoff date for registration for school is Dec 1st. My birthday is Nov 24, 1935, so I started school when I was a very immature four years old.

I dropped out of heaven reading but that's the only thing I did right. Wrestling and physical fighting with either boys or girls was my passion. And I always won. I was always ready to play war games and cops and robbers, and I lived up to the reputation of being the best "double dare" achiever.

Skates, jacks, jump rope and hopscotch were also a big part of my days, and I usually made the decisions and led the way for others to play. Needless to say I was a "tomboy" and a bully to all but the underdog whom I protected and chose to be on my teams.

Hi, my name is Peggy. Do you want to play jacks? No overs, no touches, and everything is a miss. Want to play? I got 15 jacks. Only baby's play with ten. What's your name"? "Darlene," she answered.

"Okay, let's play, and you can't catch with two hands. That is counted as a miss, and kisses is a miss too," I said. "Ha, ha, I made fun, "You can't catch the ball. You can't play if you can't catch the ball. I will show you how. No, No, now, watch. Don't throw the ball so high, Throw it straight up not out."

Recess was over, and she didn't catch one ball, but she was my new friend that I meant on the first day of school. When it was time to go home, she walked in the same direction that I did. We lived just one street apart.

I never could find anyone in kindergarten that could play jacks. My cousin Marylou was three years older than me, and she taught me good. She thought she was so smart because she always won. Well, not for long, because my goal in life was to beat her at jacks and I practiced and practiced until I could play as good as she could, and if I won, she would say I cheated and give me an Indian burn.

One day after childhood was long gone, after my children were in high school, Marylou came for an afternoon visit-not that that was unusual, it was unusual, however, that we were not at work.

I fixed lunch for her. We were reminiscing the years gone by when I said, "Hey, wanna play jacks?" She said, "Do you have some?" I said," All fifteen. Everything's a miss and no overs."

We went out on the front porch and got in our special position when the neighbor across the street walked over. "What are you guy's doing?" She asked.

"Playing jacks. Do you want to play?" I asked.

"Oh," she said, "I haven't played jacks since I was a "kid." That's okay; we haven't either, we'll let you go first it will be fun.

We thought, *"We would cream her fast".*

Well, she played all 15 hands without one mistake and named the second game. We always thought the hardest game was Double Flying Dutchman, and Marylou and I mastered that.

Our neighbor was ambidextrous and named the second game to be played with our left hand. We did not do so well. We didn't play one hand all the way through.

This is an insignificant memory but how would you like to have your championship stripped from you through a trick, instead of any real skill, like "Double Flying Dutchman?

---***---

I am just like my Mother because I have her temperament. Oh, I don't look so much like her. She was a very pretty lady with beautiful golden red hair and green eyes that turned yellow sometimes, depending on her outfit or how she was feeling. A girl at school told me that I was pretty, and I loved her forever. I had common brown hair and common blue eyes.

I am like my mother because I have her temperament. I am so much like her that one time after loosing my temper, I wondered if I was just a continuation of her and not my own person, if I was continuing her life.

My Mother was a Dorsey and had three sisters and four brothers. Their temperaments were similar, so I guess I am just a product of the Dorsey's. I am a Dorsey.

My mother was easy to make friends with; so am I. She was too sensitive; so am I. She talked too much; so do I. And she was very opinionated; so am I.

Mom never knew I was like her because I coward in her presence. No matter how old I got, she was in charge, the leader and the decision maker. She said, "Jump" and I said, "How high?"

Around my mom, I was quiet, obedient, and melancholy as much as I could be. I was scarred of my mother. She would blow up even if she assumed I was guilty and get so angry that she would switch me; I am sure I deserved most of my switching's but not as many as she gave me or as hard and long.

Not until I was in my thirties did I take a stand against her and have a yelling match. She won and slapped me good. I was in my forties before I realized that she was not only capable of lying but that she sometimes lied to me. When I was in my early teens, I thought she was a saint, and couldn't imagine how she ever got pregnant; she would never do anything that nasty.

My mother had a vicious temper. It was called "A red head's temper," and hers got out of control-with her siblings, her husband, and especially with me. Everyone loved her and I loved her the most. She was Miss sanguine to friends and neighbors, but to family she was the leader, the Choleric (Speaking of her personality type) in no uncertain terms.

The Dorsey's were a clannish family like no other. They even looked much alike. All twelve had red hair, green eyes, and freckles. What one did, the other did. They were Catholics until they came to California in the twenties, and they all became Protestants by attending Angelus Temple, a protestant church that they were invited to visit. They agreed with each other as a whole but fought over insignificant things with each other. It was not until after World War 11 that they started moving greater distances away from each other.

My mother, Julian, was diagnosed with Tuberculosis, called *consumption* in those days, when she was 10 years old. In 1925, they didn't have any antibiotics, and it was usually fatal. She was wasting away rapidly, loosing weight and bedridden.

Her mother, Ruth, had a sister that came to California a year or two before and had started going to a protestant church called Angelus Temple. She invited Ruth to go with her and ask prayer for Julian.

Normally Grandma Ruth would have never attended a church that was not Catholic, but Julian was dying, and they could do nothing for her. Grandma Ruth was willing to go with her sister to pray.

Ruth received Jesus as her personal Savior that night. The Holy Spirit touched her, and she knew her daughter was healed. Julian had a long recovery period of a year.

Chapter Three

I remember a lot even though I was just a tot. I was there and watched life in play, and sometimes I didn't want to stay. I want my Daddy. I would say, "Jesus will stop my daddy from being a drunkard someday."

I don't think there are many, if any, children that can remember much before the age of four. Maybe they can remember an incident or two, a bad thing, or a shock. I can remember a couple of incidents, or at least I think they our memories instead of the family's stories that I heard over, and over again. I might remember something one way but my older cousin might say, "No it happened another way.

What's funny is when the adult siblings get together and start to hash over one of these significant stories, most always everyone has a different view and an argument breaks out from what really took place.

How can our history books be reliable? History is a record from a historian or person about something that took place in the past, and the stories differ from each other.

I don't think there were many teachers who taught history. If they did, they sure didn't teach it like Bill O'Reilly and his research team. I have learned more history from his books then all my years in school.

My mother divorced my father, James Grabs, when I was three and in 1938, that was a stigma even though the church rules said she had proper cause.

My father was five years older then my mother. They married when she was 18. He had come to California from Texas when he was just twelve and immediately got a job in a print shop as a stock boy. There he stayed and became a Teletype operator, working all through the Great Depression.

Mom had never been employed, and she did not drive, so she was helpless after her divorce. She didn't seem to realize it, though. My Mother told me that my daddy was a drunkard, and that was why we didn't live with him any more.

When she left my father, my mother went home to her parents for some help until she could get a job and some child support. They knew her problems but told her that they could not help her that she made her bed and had to lay in it. They suggested that maybe her sister Caroline needed some help. Her husband Bernie was retired and home with the kids.

Bernie and their oldest boy did not get along, and he was ready to make Caroline quit her job. Aunt Caroline was happy indeed to take Mom, and me in exchange of taking care of their four "kids."

I do remember a few things but not much during the time we lived with Aunt Caroline and Uncle Bernie. My mom has no trouble telling the stories over and over again.

I remember vividly at age three, I grieved to see my daddy and stayed with him sometimes. I stayed a couple of weeks in the summer and a few days during Easter and Christmas, it never seemed long enough.

I never told my mother, but when I stayed with him, he took me to his special bar. He would stand me on the counter and tell me to sing, "Oh Johnny" and dance, and if I did, he would buy me a surprise. He never did. After "Oh Johnny," it was "Three Little Fishes." There was a friend of my dad's who always had his trumpet with him, and he would accompany me.

I loved doing it, I would swing my hips, gesture with my arms, and express the words with feeling. Coins and dollars were thrown on the counter for my performance, and I was the center of attention all evening. This went on until my dad put me in a booth to go to sleep, and he stayed until the last drink was served at 2:00 a.m. Children were not allowed in bars, and they couldn't serve alcohol to anyone under 21. I don't know how my father got away with this.

My own memories probably started when I was four, starting kindergarten, and some incidences that impressed me. For example, one rainy day, my four older cousins and I were playing in the house when a wrestling bout broke out, including some hard socking between Henry and Herb. One of those socks slammed right through the wall ripping the wallpaper that gave a little color to the room and covered the cockroaches that hid there during the day.

Marylou, the youngest of the four, but three years older then me, ran and got a picture from the bedroom wall and gave it to the boy's to hang over the hole hoping that it would not be noticed by their parents. It was more noticeable than the hole would have been because it was much too low to be decorated by a black and white picture.

CHAPTER FOUR

Five little monkeys' jumping on the bed; one fell off and bumped her head. Mommy called the doctor and the doctor said, "No more monkeys jumping on the bed."

*H*owe was 13 the oldest and the hardest to control. He would always come up with an irritating prank or remark to start war between Henry and Herb. Sometimes he even got Marylou involved.

Howe was never happy and soon got into some serious trouble by stealing his father's car. He headed for Las Vegas with a few dollars he took from my mother's purse. All hell broke out. He was so spoiled, a troublemaker, and nothing pleased him more than to cause a fight within the family.

Uncle Bernie reported his missing car. Howe spent six weeks in jail. Caroline would never forgive Bernie for turning his own son in.

Watching my cousins' every move, their expressions, and their mannerism taught me how to wrestle, sock, give Indian burns, and suck in my cheeks while raising my eyebrows as to say, "Ha-ha," and that is how I controlled my kindergarten class.

We lived with Mom's oldest sister, my aunt Caroline Summers, in her big old house for two or more years. She was a crass, hard-working woman, ate too much of her own cooking, and was too heavy for her small frame. She cooked and baked as a hobby, and always had something good and ready to eat.

Caroline and Mom baked bread in the evenings. After School, Henry and Herb would place the bread in their wagon and go door-to-door selling it for ten cents a loaf.

Uncle Bernie was an elderly man. He was an atheist and communist. He and Caroline had terrible arguments about going to church and worshipping Jesus. It was usually Caroline that started the argument because she wanted him to be a believer and be patriotic like she was.

The Dorsey family was very disappointed to think that their daughter married a man that did not believe in God. They considered an atheist to be evil. Uncle Paul, Virginia's husband, said, "He read too much. He was into Karl Marx, and he couldn't separate fact from fiction."

Aunt Caroline often had great family get-together and dinners. She was the glue of the family, and they all treated this so-called evil man, my uncle Bernie, so nice to his face. Don't you hate that?

I don't think we should criticize someone to another person, unless it's your spouse that would be different. It would also be different if you sincerely needed to talk to someone because you have been hurt and don't know what to do. And I think it is fun to have debates on something we have been reading or researching.

Why, oh why can't we control our evil tongue? Uncle Bernie had a tender heart, and he was every good to me. He taught me how to play checkers, and I could beat my cousins when I could get them to play with me. Marylou didn't count because she was always available to play. She didn't play very well and would say I cheated and then give me an Indian burn.

Mom took care of Caroline and Bernie's four "Kids" and me, which made five little monkeys. She did the house chores, to include the washing and ironing, for our board and room.

Aunt Caroline was a cook in a downtown restaurant. Uncle Bernie was retired and stayed home. He was never a bother, nor did he help. He was always there but stayed busy inventing something or trying to. So he kept to himself and out of a helpful position.

Things would go fairly well for a while, and then Mom and Aunt Caroline would get into a tremendous fight over one of her little monkeys. Those fights usually ended up with Mom dragging me out of the house with a bag of our belongings and no place to go. She said that we would have to sleep in neighborhood parked cars until she got a job.

We never slept in a parked car. Uncle Bernie would come after us. He would side in with Mom in a way that she could save her pride and come back in the house. All the little monkeys were told not to jump on the bed again, and they didn't – until the next incident, that is.

CHAPTER FIVE

Oh where, oh where can sister Aimee be? Oh where, oh where can she be? With the press at their best, they could only guess where Sister Aimee could be.

*M*y Mother meant Jim Grabs, my father, at Angelus Temple, a famous church in Los Angelus, where he wooed her playing gospel songs on the piano. After their divorce, she meant my stepfather there also, as this was her church.

Aimee Semple McPhersons was the founder and pastor of this famous church. "Sister Aimee," as she was called, was a successful itinerant (traveling) evangelist.

She arrived in Los Angeles in 1918 but continued to travel and raise money for her vision to build the large domed church in the metropolitan Echo Park area of Los Angeles. The sanctuary had a seating capacity of 5,300 people that was filled three times a day, seven days a week. It was known as the Foursquare Gospel and became a mainstream Pentecostal denomination.

Sister Aimee blended contemporary culture with Christianity. Many Christian churches today try to blend contemporary culture with Christianity, and find it to be a very difficult task. Some call themselves "nondenominational," but the pastors could have credentials from a religion that you know nothing about. Usually though, they are from a mainstream Protestant church.

A Nondenominational church sounds wonderful. No way can anyone be offended (Snowflake?) Yes? No? These churches are doing very well in today's culture, which perhaps today's culture could be defined as "One big Compromise"

Angelus Temple was dedicated on January1, 1923, and Sister Aimee would be its full-time pastor, taking advantage of radio. Her station was the very first Christian radio station. Angelus Temple had a twenty-four hour prayer tower, movies and stage plays. One time for a stage act, Sister Aimee rode to the pulpit on a motorcycle. She employed artists, decorators, electricians and carpenters to build sets for each Sunday service. That's not so unique today but it was in her day.

Many famous actors & actresses could not resist coming to hear and see Sister Aimee, even if their own church forbade visiting another denomination. She was not only famous, but she was beautiful. How can a beautiful, intelligent, successful, and famous woman live in this fallen world without a slip-up? Could there be just one?

Sister Aimee no longer toured, at least not until May 18,1926, when at the height of her popularity, she vanished. No one had a clue where she was, and her congregation held a memorial service for her. There were many stories of what happened and "Fake News" with their scandalous stories was raking in the dough, re. Me. Where oh where did sister Aimee go?

She showed up on June 23. Not to long of a journey, she stumbled out of the desert in Agua Prieta, Sonora, and a Mexican town across the border from Douglas, Arizona. She claimed she had been kidnapped and held for ransom. Ma, ma said, "Not likely."

I don't think about Sister Aimee's sensational disappearance as a reason to write her off as a fraud. In the classic book *The Pilgrim's Progress* (Paul Bunion), the character, Christian, stumbled off the right path, fell on to a path that led to destruction but was saved with the right persuasion to get back on to the right path. With a repenting heart he did, and with determination, he reached his destination.

The world's thorny switch did a number on Sister Aimee, and she suffered the consequences of her disappearance until her death in 1944. The coroner said she died of an accidental overdose of sleeping pills and pain pills compounded by kidney failure. But Sister Aimee did a mighty work after she came back. A mighty work indeed: In 1936 Sister Aimee opened a commissary at Angelus Temple. It was open twenty-four hours a day, seven days a week. She had a soup kitchens and free clinics during the Great Depression.

When World War 11 broke out she became involved in the peoples needs to endure. Sister Aimee included war bond rallies and sermons that linked the church with American patriotism.

Aimee Semple McPherson's story is interesting and has played an important part in my life. The Foursquare church was our denomination and my mother wanted to live by their rules. Her husbands did not and she always felt guilty for the life she lived. My mother used to say, "Do as I say, not as I do."

CHAPTER SIX

The Five Little Monkeys' stopped jumping on the bed. Four of those monkeys wished a man dead. The fifth little monkey who bumped her head moved to a house with her Mother and Ted.

*U*ncle Bernie passed away, and Aunt Caroline was grieved. But time took care of that.

It wasn't long before my mother meant Theodore Tucker from church. She knew his sister, Irene, from school, so their relationship instantly grew as they shared "Do you remember?" acquaintances.

Ted was a talented artist. He could draw portraits and paint them to look alive. He was a melancholy man but seldom moody as most melancholy people are. He was very neat and reserved– until he had a beer, that is. One beer and he became a dancer. Two beers and he became a singer, tumbler and piano player. After four beers, he became a sanguine and took center stage.

Ted wooed Mom with his talents, and even though he was only five-foot-three, she considered him to be handsome and very intelligent.

They were married in 1939. I have read that because we are attracted to a particular temperament or personality, it is common that we remarry the same type of person as the first time. My Mother married another alcoholic, but she could control this second one better, she thought. Mom was a controller, but in many ways she was the one out of control. She was sometimes like an untamed lioness, and her bluff was vicious and desperate.

Now Mom was pregnant and her baby was due in the summer 1941 She had s little girl, a blue baby and she died a few hours after birth. Mom took it very hard, and her doctor suggested that she get pregnant again right away. She did and had a beautiful baby boy in April of 1942.

Ted's sister, Irene, was divorced and left with three boys who were very close to my age. Bobby, Larry and Jimmy. We were four of a wild kind.

Their father, Bob, was a Western Singer on radio. He was tall, blonde, handsome, and a real womanizer.

He was not paying child support regularly. Irene was having a hard time making it, so her boys were shuffled back and forth between their father and her. Sometimes the boys were separated, meaning one lived with an aunt another with someone else until their parents could take them back. They had the world's thorny switch on them from the time they were born.

Bobby, the oldest boy, became a Marine in "The Forgotten War"– you know, the one wedged in between World War 11 and the Vietnam War. The Korean War started when North Korea invaded South Korea– that one.

Thousands of American soldiers lost their lives in that war, and there are over seven thousand American soldiers unaccounted for. Bobby was shot down by friendly fire. He had to have a metal Plate over his chest cavity and was not expected to live. He became an alcoholic and died in his forties.

Soon after Mom married Ted, his father, Ralph, showed up, down and out, without a place to live or a car to drive. He always had enough change in his pocket for a bottle of Jack Daniels or a couple of six packs and cigarettes that he earned doing concession work at the racetracks.

He was a short man, squarely built and very neat, permanently dressed in a suit, tie, and a felt hat. Aunt Caroline thought he was the cat's meow and he knew she did.

The courtship was on, and they were married with-in six months of their first date. Ralph, my new grandpa, moved in with Aunt Caroline, my mother, my new step-daddy, and us five little monkeys.

None of the kids called Ralph "Dad"; he was just "Ralph."

Maybe he did not want to be called Dad. Maybe the kids' bad manners embarrassed their new father. They and I were unsophisticated, untidy, and our table manners were gross. Our vocabulary consisted of words and phrases that only the Dorsey family could interpret.

I did not have to call him "Grandpa," either, just Ralph. I did have to call Ted, Daddy,"but I didn't mind. I referred to my father as my "real daddy."

Ralph immediately thought he would take his new family in hand. He started picking first on their table manners.

I thought Henry and Herb ate with style, I loved to watch them eat breakfast. Henry was always reading a book with one hand with his other scooping up egg yolk with his toast. He made it look so good. Herb devoured comic books while he spooned in corn flakes without looking at his bowl or spoon. After they left for school, I went for their leftovers.

Ralph made his first big mistake when he showed disproval of the boy's table manners. It was the way he did it that angered Caroline and embarrassed everyone else.

Sunday afternoon, we were all sitting at the table. Aunt Caroline had prepared a roast. She served mashed potatoes and gravy with all the trimmings that go with a perfect Sunday dinner. After saying the blessing, Ralph dropped his head down to his plate and started licking his dinner. He took his hand and shoveled some gravy in his mouth, letting it drool back on to his plate. He was drunk.

Everyone was shocked, sitting straight in our chairs and staring at him. He gave out a couple of loud belches and said, "What's wrong? That's the way you kids eat.

Caroline said, "If you don't like the way my kids eat, then don't pretend that you enjoy being with us so much. If you don't like it, go dine somewhere else." And then she turned his plate upside down. What a mess!

What a beautiful dinner that didn't get eaten because everyone was shocked and upset. We had the mashed potatoes as potato patties for breakfast, and we had the roast beef for sandwiches latter that evening. The vegetables were saved for the next dinner meal.

Ted was embarrassed and became very quiet. He walked outside with Mom, and I followed.

It was a perfect afternoon. There were enough clouds in the sky to partly shade the sun, and there was just a tiny breeze. It made me want to stay out on the porch forever.

Ted said that we needed to get our own place. It wasn't right that we were on top of each other all the time. Even though we were paying our own way, we needed to be alone.

Aunt Caroline's four little monkeys were delighted with the dinner. Their attitude was, "Drop dead Ralph" and their checks were sucked in, eyebrows raised and chin pointed to the ceiling.

From that evening on, Ralph continued to pick on the kids but in quite a different way. He was less expressive and more courteous in the way he corrected them. My cousins hated Ralph, and little things started happening to him. Such as, one evening he fell asleep on the front pouch swing, drunk as usual. Caroline aroused him from his sleep to find his ankles and legs covered in little red ants, which lived around the area and whose bites were very plentiful. Ralphs ankles became puffy and red to where he couldn't get his shoes on.

One thing after another happened to Ralph, the kids would hide his hat or his glasses, and swear that they didn't take them. One time he was sitting at the table, and the back leg of the chair he was sitting on gave away. He didn't get hurt because the chair didn't completely collapse. He claimed that the leg was obviously loosened on purpose because the other three legs were not loose at all.

Despite all the mishaps and grumbling, he and Caroline were lovers, and in front of her he was nice to the little monkeys.

CHAPTER SEVEN

Seashells and a dead starfish are in my pail. Closed clams in my hand and barefoot all day in the sand. Pearl Abalone shells to place on my ear and listen to the sea all year.

*T*ed, my stepfather, was close to the same age as my mother, and he was never employed full-time during the Great Depression, few were. He did odd jobs that he could find and even had a couple of tumbling gigs in Hollywood.

He spent time in the Civilian Conservation Corps (CCC camps) that President Roosevelt founded for the relief of unemployment.

The CCC camps operated under the army's control. The work was soil preservation and replantation of trees. The organization planted millions of trees. Many were planted in areas that were made barren by fires. They built over thirty thousand wildlife shelters.

They stocked rivers and lakes with fish. Within less then ten years, they did work that was insurmountable with a group of young unmarried men that worked for $35 to $45 a month building roads, bridges, and parks and every worthwhile project to make America's topography Great.

Incredibly and unexpectedly, these men were being prepared for the massive call of civilians for World War 11. They were in shape and ready to go. Ted was able to claim two children and was not called for duty until 1944.

Soon he found employment with Lockheed Inc. as a bookkeeper. He found a little house for us to rent just a couple of blocks from Aunt Caroline's.

My new daddy, not my real one, was so much fun. He was happy and filled the house with music. His paintings and drawings covered the walls, and he loved to go places and do things. He took us to the "Show" (movies) at least once a week but sometimes twice.

Ted liked to play pinochle with their friends, and takes drives in the evening. His favorite place was the beach, and he taught us how to enjoy it without spending much money. We went camping before most people knew how because going through the Great Depression left little thought of vacations. I told him when I grew up I was going to marry him.

Ted and his sister didn't suffer so much during the Depression. Even though his parents were divorced, their mother was a seamstress and did housework.

Mother said that Irene always had hi-heels, silk stockings and plenty of dates to keep her entertained.

Now Irene had there boys that she could not support and she didn't know what to do. Ted and my Mom invited her to move in with us until she got a full-time job and Bob started paying child support. Irene was thrilled and helped with the groceries. She worked part-time at an insurance Co. But continually worried about being laid off; insurance was not a necessity in those days.

Irene was as talented as her brother, Ted, and she expressed it in crafts and sewing. Everything she touched turned out beautiful.

She was like Ted in that she hated the routine of a forty-hour job and she couldn't find one in her talents anyway. She always ended up doing office work with low pay– not enough money to support three boys.

Irene was very intelligent like her brother. She was married twice and divorced twice. She had always lived with her mother and didn't have to worry so much about rent and utilities. Now she will be living with her brother and her boy's and she was thrilled. She loved her boys, but she couldn't find a way to support them, and she didn't.

CHAPTER EIGHT

Bobby, Larry, what shall we do? Put out this fire or it will burn you. Peggy quick, throw me my shoes, and we'll break the window and jump through.

*B*obby, Larry, Jimmy and I had so much fun together. There was never a fight between us. But we were very mischievous and we never wound down. What one didn't think of, another did.

Our new rented little house had only two bedrooms, but there was a small wooden shed close to the house. It wasn't attached and there was no entryway from the shed leading into the house. It became a detached bedroom for the two oldest boys and me. It was large enough for bunk beds and a twin.

It had its own window that was on the same side where the bunk beds had been placed, and it had a door to the outside.

The adults locked the window and door so we couldn't get out. During one particular night, on the way to our newly decorated bedroom, I picked up a book of matches to play with.

The door was locked, the room was dark, and we three played boogieman until we scarred each other, pulled the covers over our head, and made howling noises with laughter. I decided to strike the matches that I had brought along to play with. The first match didn't light, the second match didn't light, but the third lit all the rest of the matches in the pack. They burnt my fingers, so I threw them, and they landed at the bottom of my bed.

The blanket caught fire, which raced back toward me, I ran to the bunk beds screaming, and Bobby, the oldest, started hitting the window. It wouldn't break. Then he kicked it and kicked it and hit it with his shoe, and it broke all jagged.

Both boys were smashing the window. Larry was the first one out. He had cuts all over the sides of his hands around to the end of his first finger because he had doubled up his fist to pound the window. When he jumped, he landed on shattered glass. The bottom of his feet and hands had tiny pieces of glass imbedded in them. It took days before he could walk without it feeling like pins were in his feet.

Bobby then took my arms, and helped me slide down the side of the shed, and let go. I also got glass imbedded in my feet. My hand was not blistered, but burnt and very red.

Bobby was last. He had two deep cuts on each of his underarms right by his armpits, received when he was lowering me down. His hands were all scratched with tiny cuts. His hair, eyebrows, and face were covered with glass.

Before we saw anyone, we heard the fire trucks. Smoke was belching up puffs, and the fire was a blaze. The neighbors and our landlord were out watching.

My mother and Aunt Irene, in their nightgowns with their hair set in pin curls, and Ted in his shorts and a t-shirt were screaming and running toward us.

The fire was rapidly put out. The shed was completely destroyed, and the corner of the house was burned. There was a lot of smoke damage as well as water damage caused by the firemen.

This long frightening night was not over. We were checked and our wounds washed. No ambulance came for us, and we were not taken to the doctor. Irene cleaned Bobby's cuts and stopped the bleeding. Mama put my hands and feet in cold water. And she brushed the glass off us. I told them what I had done, and the landlord was furious, he kicked us out.

He screamed at my mother and said that I was a brat. He said that he was going to sue us. Mom said, "Go ahead. You can't get blood out of a turnip." What ever that meant.

The landlord said to Ted, "You told me that you only had one child. The house would be for you, your wife, and one child. That shed was not to be used as a room. It was for storage."

He was frantic and wouldn't shut up. Them my mother started screaming back to him. She told him that the rent was paid up and he was to get out of their house.

There was too much smoke for us to stay there for the night, so Irene and the boy's went to her mother's apartment, and Ted, Mom, and me went to Aunt Caroline's.

The landlord must have had insurance because he never sued, and we never heard from him again. Soon after that, Irene's boys went back with their father, and Ted started looking for another house to rent.

Grandma Dorsey had just become a widow and still had much life to live. After Grandpa died, she moved in with her next-to-oldest daughter, Virginia and Paul Keys and their seven-year-old daughter, Pauline, who was the same age as Marylou. It was a nice arrangement. They got along well. Grandma did a lot of sewing for Pauline and by far did her share of chores. On some weekends, Paul loved to take his family, including the cousins, to the beach or a large park with a swimming pool. He saw to it that we had enough food and drinks to last all day and into the evening. He worked at Lockheed too and sometimes moonlighted in the concession stands in the Los Angeles Coliseum.

Grandma meant Archibald Bell at church, his wife had died, and soon, after a very short courtship, he and Grandma were married. Now I had another Grandpa: Grandpa Ralph, my step-daddy's father, and Grandpa Archie. My mother never instructed that I call either one of them Grandpa, and I was told to just call them by their first name. Maybe they did not want to be called Grandpa. All the kids just called them by their first name.

Archie rented a one-bedroom apartment for him and Grandma just a few blocks away from Aunt Virginia, which made her very happy, and they were just four streets from Aunt Caroline's. If not together, the whole Dorsey family– Mom's mother, brothers, and sisters– always lived close to one another.

CHAPTER NINE

"I got a secret," a four-year old might say. "Do you know my secret? She will giggle, and say, "I can't tell you my secret today."

We were all visiting Aunt Caroline one Saturday. Some were sitting in the living room and some outside when I decided to see what smelled so good in the kitchen.

Archie was in there bouncing a ball as though he were waiting for me to play with him. He said, "Sit down and I will roll the ball to you." I did. He said, "Spread your legs." I did. "Farther, and pull your dress up so you can catch the ball with your legs." I did.

He rolled the ball hard; I could not catch the ball with my legs. Instead it hit my pee-pee (my vagina). I rolled it back. He did it again and said, "doesn't that feel good?" Then asked me to come and sit on his lap.

But then he heard someone coming and He said, "Hush. This game is our secret. You are not to tell anyone about it, and if you do I will hurt your Mother real bad." I was barely four and I didn't understand, yet I did, I knew it was bad and I can remember a nauseating feeling rush over me. I became very quiet. I wondered why he would hurt Mama.

My mother told me that if I did something bad and I told her before Jesus did I wouldn't get in as much trouble and probably wouldn't get a spanking.

I believed that with all of my heart, and I told her everything that I thought was bad to the point of her being irritated. But now I was very quiet and scared. What if Jesus tells her about the game? I told Jesus I would never play that game again if He would just not tell my mother. I didn't understand the game, not for a long, time.

Ted and my mother were looking for a house to rent and they found one in the same neighborhood as aunt Caroline's. It was a two-bedroom, a miniature backyard, and a huge front yard, and a garage.

I would be starting first grade at the same school. I loved the "kids" in my kindergarten class. They obeyed my every command because I could read. Only one other girl in our class could read but not as good as I could.

I could play jacks, and roller skate with eight ball barring's in each wheel and they couldn't-not yet-anyway and I gave Indian burns for their submission.

I was very excited that I passed kindergarten. My teacher was not all that happy with me. She told my Mother that I was too bossy, talked too much in class, and made a couple of the children cry. She suggested that they make a playhouse for me to play in for the summer months. She thought that would better prepare me for first grade by learning how to play quietly by myself.

Except for the chickenpox and the most horrible, horrific incident, I had the most wonderful summer in store for me and my step daddy bought me my first puppy.

Even though the summer had started on the day I got my puppy, it was sprinkling, unheard of in June. We named the puppy Sprinkles. She was white with black spots and black freckles on her noise. She had long hair and long ears she was so beautiful. Unfortunately Mom couldn't potty train her, so I didn't get to keep her for very long. Mom felt sorry for me, so I told her it was okay because I had many dog friends on my skating route that I traveled everyday but none as beautiful as Sprinkles.

CHAPTER TEN

I was just a little girl, helpless as could be, I saw a sight that frightened me, and I tried to take flight from that horrifying sight. I was caught, but I screamed and fought and ran from Archie's evil plot.

This summer day was hot, and all the kids were running through the sprinklers in their front yard. I had turned five and was too young to be left alone without a sitter. Mom was going to court over my child support that my Father was not paying.

Ted had to work. Mom couldn't drive, and she didn't want to go alone. Her sister, Virginia, was anxious to drive her because she wanted to see a courtroom. Grandma had never seen a courtroom and wanted to go with them. Archie offered to watch me.

I never forgot about the secret game. I was afraid of him, but I didn't exactly know why, and I couldn't tell anyone.

I was outside playing with the neighbor Kids. I heard Archie calling me, but I pretended not to hear as long as I could. He yelled for me with some authority and anger in his voice this time. I came running into the house to find him sitting in a chair with the front of his pants open with his humongous, enormous penis standing erect out of his pants into the air.

He grabbed me tried to pull me to it. He said, "Touch it." I screamed so loud that it scared him, enough that he lost his grip on me. He said," you tell anyone, I will kill your mother."

I pulled away from him and ran. We lived within walking distance of the Los Angeles River, and that's where I ran.

I hid behind some bushes for a long while. I was so scared. I didn't know when Mom would be home, and I couldn't tell her anyway.

I pondered the situation, I thought about what I had seen and was fixated on it. *I saw a baby penis. Mom told me that boys had a penis and girls didn't. I saw my cousin's penis one time. We played "You show me yours and I'll show you mine." That didn't scare me. I thought it was fun.*

Some how kids just know it's wrong to play that way so I told my mom before Jesus could. She told me not to ever do that again, that it was nasty and good little girls never played that game.

I was thinking it all out. I had never saw anything like that– not yet. I was only five. I was afraid to go home, but if I was gone when Mom, Aunt Virginia, and Grandma returned and Archie says he called for me and I wouldn't come in, they will come looking for me with a switch.

I waited a long time before I left my hiding place at the river but I knew it was time to get home. When I got back, they were still not home, so I waited across the street and talked to Mrs. Combo while she watered her plants until I saw Aunt Virginia pull in the drive way.

If houses can be possessed I think ours was. One night I woke up with spiders in my bed, crawling on my feet and legs. I screamed and screamed, Mom said I was just dreaming, but I saw them. They were real, and she could not quiet me down until they disappeared. They never came back but I can still see them in my mind.

Ted never had to pay rent and utilities and buy food before. He had always stayed with his mother, was in the C.C.C. Camps, or living with friends, And any money he earned was his spending money.

Ted was a narcissist. He was a dreamer, an artist, a tumbler, a lover of nature and the outdoors, a fascinating man, and lazy when it came to any kind of work that did not fit into his talents.

He was twenty-four when he married Mom. His sister had invited him to church to meet her, and my mother was an instant novelty to him. She was beautiful and her golden red hair was long and gorgeous, perfect to draw and then paint in oils.

She was twenty-three, Miss sanguine and when he saw her, she was with a group of her followers, a group of friends singing hymns, and she was leading them into whispering and vocal twitters.

Mom had no melancholy in her. She never lived in a depressed state. She was always in an emotional state of joy or anger, depending on the crowd. Her friends never saw her display of anger unless it was to represent their cause, and then it would be theatrical.

She was a natural actress and she exercised her talent at any whim that would benefit the cause. She could fake unconsciousness, cry with real tears, play the forlorn or heartbroken or any emotion that God bestowed for man. She made the "Barrymore's" look like beginners.

Mom said she would never marry again, as most say after a divorce. Within a year she was moonstruck and absolutely fascinated with Ted.

She connected with and approved of his dreams. She scrutinized his art without criticism and with only approval, and she gave him the attention that he so desired. They were in love, and thy got married.

Ted went to church with Mom but also took her dancing and dinning to movies and the beach, which she had never done. Her church and her family thought those things were sinful. Ted said that was silly, that he believed in God and salvation, but he would never allow the church to rule his life.

He respectfully responded to her beliefs by expressing his own and why he believed the way he did.

Mom relented theatrically but not sincerely, not down deep. She brushed her discomfort aside and learned how to dance and dine in nice restaurants and smoke cigarettes like the Hollywood actress did.

When they stayed home, Ted liked to listen to music, draw portraits, and drink a six-pack of beer. If he didn't pass out, he would want to go buy another six-pack. Mom would hide his keys so he couldn't go. He would be furious and start cussing her out. Mom would become angry but control her need to attack him. She would go to bed upset and hurt.

Ted wouldn't go to bed until all his beer was gone, and Mom went through hell getting him up in the morning.

No matter how he felt, Ted wanted a large breakfast. He said that was the most important meal of the day. He started off with tomato juice. Mom fixed him scrapple with sausage and eggs, or pancakes with eggs, or bacon and eggs with fried potatoes. Every morning he would choose which combination he wanted and Mom would fix it for him.

He wanted cream for his coffee and real butter for his toast. He didn't get that, it wasn't rationed yet, but he couldn't afford it. In fact, he found his pay cheek was not sufficient to support a family and indulge in his luxurious way of life.

Nevertheless, that summer was wonderful. Mom and Ted decided I didn't need a playhouse to learn how to play more quietly since I spent two weeks in my bedroom with the chickenpox; that was enough quiet time.

We lived less than 20 miles from the cost, and all summer we spent the weekends there. We sometimes camped out and roasted marshmallows when the sun went down. Ted told us that next summer we would take a week's vacation and go to the beautiful Oregon coast.

He told us stories about Luis and Clark, but the best ones for me was about trees that you could drive through, and a tree that was a house. He talked about the California gold rush, and how fun it would be for us to pan for gold with a pie pan. He said that we would see seals, and whales and the Trees of Mystery, the oldest trees in the world.

Ted said that the California Indians never had to worry about the weather because it was always warm enough, and that shelter was no problem. Food was plentiful and California had everything for the perfect life.

Mom said that they were very smart to settle in California, and wondered how they survived in colder or warmer states. They didn't have houses like we do now, and it would be so hard to stay warm. She said she

BEVERLY MCCOY (HARLOW)

loved Southern California, and would never leave it. It was such a wonderful day; we were so contented and happy. But it seems like the worlds thorny switch makes all good things come to an end.

CHAPTER ELEVEN

Little girls are made of sugar and spice and every thing nice. I was a little girl made of sorrow and fright because of what happened some days and some nights.

*S*ummer was over, and I began first grade with new school dresses and new school shoes. To my surprise, and Mom's too, my kindergarten teacher was now my first grade teacher. Most of the same kids were in my class, and we just picked up where we left off. I loved school. I was the boss.

It seemed as though every penny Ted brought home was budgeted for necessities, and he was working harder than he ever had. He was getting restless and bored of the repetitiveness. Instead of his Julian wanting to go dancing with him, she wanted to save every penny for a new baby on the way and besides that she was always sick.

She was sick at the beginning of her pregnancy, which was at the end of the summer months, and she couldn't fix Ted's breakfast. The smell of food made her nauseous and caused her to vomit. The doctor says that morning sickness usually stops after the embryo period, and you retain some strength. Mom had morning sickness only during that time, but it seemed forever.

Her nausea and running to the bathroom a hundred times a day to throw up or pee was very unromantic to young, energetic Ted that wanted to be pampered.

Ted seemed to become un-happy with his life and with Julian. He felt like a trapped animal, and he wanted to be free and have Julian back as his beautiful sanguine lover. Instead he has to suffer another pregnancy with her, and be responsible for her kid, who demanded most of the attention in the house, not to mention her expense.

Ted didn't want a house or babies, but he did want Julian, the way she was when he'd married her. If they could just indulge in what nature has to offer-no routine, live life without materialism– they could be happy forever, he thought.

He was not content any more, and he began to criticize everything, to include Mom's cooking. He criticized how we folded his clothes. He wanted them folded a certain way and placed in his drawer a certain way.

We were never to get in his drawers except to put his clothes away. He was very neat, Mom never had to pick up after him.

Ted thought a piano should be in every home, and he spent time looking for a good used one. He could talk Julian into giving him some money she had saved for the new baby. No matter how small the amount of money Mom got her hands on she would always save some. The baby wasn't due until April and he would get a raise before then. He could get the piano now and it would also serve as our Christmas gifts to each other.

This beautiful up right with real ivory keys barley fit in our living room, but it became the centerpiece of our little spotless house. The piano occupied Ted's restlessness for hours on into the night. He used the piano the same way as he did his art, and now he had two hobbies that he loved to indulge in at the same time. He would have a drawing or a painting set up in the living room, a can of beer open on the end table for him to reach and swill from. In between art strokes, he would play the piano. He lived in his own imaginary world.

But that was not enough. The dreamier Ted felt, the more he enjoyed the feeling he obtained from alcohol. He continued his beer drinking and criticizing. He started improving my table manners by criticizing them at each meal, usually just one or two things per meal.

I never felt that he was picking on me. I thought I was special to him because he became my second daddy. It never occurred to me that he was discussed with my manners and me. I would follow his instruction, but for just the one meal. By the next meal, I'd forgotten all that he'd taught me-not on purpose; I just didn't think about it.

Ted never said the blessing, so I usually rushed into a conversation about my day before they had a chance to talk about their day or ask me about mine.

Poor Ted. I am sure it was frustrating for him because I wasn't really his daughter. Teaching me manners was just a game. It would be hard to correct someone else's kid, especially one that was showering him with affection.

The best instruction was that I was to chew each bite ten times before I swallowed. I would count and swallow.

I thought it was fun and remembered to do it two or three times, getting Mom and Ted's attention as I expressed each chew. The attention didn't last long, so I was back to one, two, three gulp. Ted told me to a sit up straight and keep my elbows off the table. That was hard because I always slouched and had my elbows on the table like Henry and Herb. At one meal, he told me to put my knife on the back of my plate after using it and to keep my mouth closed while chewing. My Mother spoke up and said, "Ted quit picking on her at every meal."

He said I am not picking on her. I am teaching her some manners. How can she learn to hold her fork proper with her little pinky finger up in the air (he demonstrated) the way she eats? His little finger popped up in the air, and looked so funny that we started laughing. I still don't have good table manners, but I sometimes hold my pinky finger up in the air just like a lady should.

I always needed shoes, not just because I was growing but the clamps from my skates pulled the soles away from the tops and I usually had a rubber band holding them together.

It seemed to Ted that I always needed something such as milk money for school. I didn't always get that. A lot kids didn't because most people were going through tough times, just beginning to come out of the Depression.

The school requested a blanket for us to lie on the floor. In kindergarten and first grade, we received a graham cracker and milk at 10:00 a.m. lie down on our blanket, and closed our eyes for fifteen minutes or for whatever time was allotted. I also needed a raincoat and galoshes because I walked to school.

Ted was right. It seemed like every payday something was needed for Peggy or the new baby that was on its way.

Mom was trying to control Ted's drinking, and what time he was to go to bed so he would get up in the morning. As a result, they began to argue routinely.

Ted would sometimes not come home from work but instead go out for a beer with one or two of the guys. There was no such thing as having a couple of beers. He would drink until he was in a drunken stupor and drive himself home. The word *intoxicated* cannot describe with the right emphasis his drunken stupors. How he ever got home each time is miraculous. Luckily, he never got in an accident or received a ticket.

Julian was always furious. She was also worried that Ted's behavior would soon cause him to lose his job. He already had three warnings for being late and took a reduction of some hours off his paycheck.

In terms of the pregnancy, Mom started feeling better, she began making baby clothes, she didn't have a sewing machine, but she would hand stich them together and use her sister's machine when she got the chance.

Nearly every day, Mom took a long walk along the river. There was a pass that leads right to Dolly Madison's little bakery. Bear claws were her favorite, with one of those and a cup of coffee, she could dream and plan for her new baby and take her mind off Ted's drinking and his unwillingness to get up in the morning.

One time she was pondering her situation and she thought, *"He has worked steady for a year. After all Peggy is not his and James hasn't paid a penny for her support, and Ted has been good to us.*" The court say's that James is obligated to pay so much a month child support, but he don't, and they never garnished his check because he has a new wife and baby to support.

Mom would tell me how lucky we were that Ted worked everyday to feed us. He bought me new dresses and new shoes for school, and I should be appreciative toward him.

I was as appreciative as a little girl knew how to be. I liked my new dresses to wear to school, and I told Ted, "Thank you."

I was six years old, and I got news that I had a new baby sister named Sarah Jean from my real daddy. Jean is my middle name. I was thrilled.

I just didn't know if I could wait until Christmas vacation before seeing her. I asked Mom if I could spend a weekend with my dad and new baby, and she said no. Christmas vacation would be here before I knew it.

She said that we were going to visit Uncle Merle, Aunt Sadie & your cousin Brian McCall. Maybe they would allow you to use their phone to call your Father and ask all about the new baby.

Uncle Merle worked for the Union Pacific Railroad. During World War 11 all railroad employees were to have phones because of emergencies. Phones were a luxury and few people had them until after the war.

My father and Step mother lived in Grandma Grab's rooming house, and rooming houses always had a phone. I still remember the phone number: (RI 0533)

It was October, and my immature anticipation of Christmas vacation visit filled my air. My jubilant, overjoyed planning and chatting about it were becoming intolerable to Ted. He was working his ass off, feeding me, clothing me, teaching me table manners, and tolerating my chatter without receiving a cent from Mr. Grabs.

Mom needed a sewing machine to finish my birthday gift she was making for me: a skirt to fit around my little make-up vanity. Gladys (Mrs. Combo to me), our neighbor across the street and Mom's friend, invited her over one evening to use her sewing machine so she could finish the skirt and they could visit.

Mrs. Combo had a daughter a year younger than me, and we often skated the neighborhood together. She could skate as good as me and didn't like to play with dolls either, so we were friends.

I always had to go to bed by 7:30 p.m. on school nights; I was already in bed and asleep when Mom went over to Gladys that evening.

Ted got undressed and put his robe on his naked body leaving it open. He got into bed with me and woke me up by putting his hand under the covers and pulling my nightgown up. He said, "Just hold still". He put his hand on my vagina and rubbed. I cried out and he said just lay still, this is what we do when we love each other. This will forever be our secret and you must never tell your Mother or anyone, if you do I will kill your mother and you." He got up and left.

SHATTERED

I wanted my Daddy– my real Daddy. I will tell him what Ted had done and said. Maybe I can live with him, but my mother will not let me, and I don't want to leave her forever. If I tell my daddy and he tells my mother, Ted will kill her and me.

Ted announced that he would have his year in by December and was thinking of taking us on our Oregon vacation for Christmas. The baby was due in April, and they wouldn't want to take their new baby on a long trip that summer.

He was not in the least bit worried about the winter weather. They had a 1938 or 39 Willis, a good car. Lockheed agreed for his vacation to be in December since he had gotten his first year in and he got two weeks' vacation instead of one by using some accumulated sick leave, and a paid holiday.

No, I didn't want to go. I wanted to stay with my daddy for Christmas. But Mom said I couldn't, that I could spend two or three weekends with him when we got back.

That is another thing that really pissed Ted off. He would say, "Mr. Grabs drinks too much to drive. He can't pick his own daughter up for visitation, and I am expected to drive his daughter to his house for his visitation."

The last time my father had driven, he was drunk and drove right through his mother's garage. He took the streetcar to work, or any other place they wanted to go after that. My stepmother was an alcoholic too, and she didn't drive.

I am so grateful that Ted drives me over and picks me up when it's time to visit my daddy. If Ted didn't I would not be able to see my father. One time my daddy came for me on the bus. We had a long walk from the bus to catch the streetcar, and he said it was too far. Next time we would take a taxi. That never happened.

I just learned that daddy was really Santa Clause. Mama said that I was lucky because I had two daddies, so there was no way Santa would not find me Christmas Eve. I didn't want two daddies' I just wanted mine.

Anyway, we would be home from our vacation three or four days before Christmas, and we would have Christmas dinner with Aunt Caroline, Ralph, and all my cousins.

Ted wanted to go on vacation early December, so they took me out of school before Christmas break started.

He had to have a break from his boring job. He couldn't take the humdrum much longer.

We were heading North to Oregon in December of 1941.

CHAPTER TWELVE

"Daddy, your window is down, and the wind is blowing all around. I'm cold," I said. My hair is blowing all over my head. "There's a blanket on the seat. Cover up and you'll get some heat. We are by the sea, by the sea, oh, the beautiful cold, cold sea.

*T*ed always wanted the window down to keep the fumes out. I used to get carsick. He said that fumes leaked into the back seat from the exhaust pipe and that was why.

On our second day December 7, 1941, we stopped at a mom and pop store and gas station for gas and some groceries for lunch. There were a lot of people gathered around the radio inside. A lady was sobbing, another comforting her. Everyone was all excited and jabbering.

What's going on? "Japanese bombed Pearl Harbor at 7:55 this morning."

Ted became terrified he thought that the entire Pacific coast was under attack. I don't know how far north we had gotten, but we gassed up and headed south for home.

We didn't have a radio in the car, so we didn't know what was happening until we stopped again for gas. We never stopped to play by the sea, and I don't remember if we stopped to sleep, but we ate the rest of our meals in the car until we got home.

All the way home, Ted cursed Admiral Yamamoto. He said that he was a stupid yellow-bellied son of a bitch. He told us that problems had been stewing with Japan for a long time because we had been sending supplies to Brittan to support the cause.

I don't think Mom knew much about current events, and Ted was really scaring her.

She knew she was not living for the Lord, and she immediately thought that it was going to be the end of the World and she was going to hell.

Ted said, "Don't be silly" and proceeded in explaining that Great Britain was at war against Germany. Hitler had taken over Germany, and his followers were called Nazis.

Ted knew everything, He read all the time, and Mama said that he was very intelligent.

Most city people in the 30's & 40's struggled to keep food on the table and very few kept up with what was going on in Europe. Most that did were men, not women. They read the newspaper and listened to the radio if they had one.

Ted said that no body really knew when the war started. The United States was not actively in the war, but we supplied material for Britain, who was and had been pressuring Japan to halt its military expansion in Asia and the Pacific.

He said they never quit fighting over there; it's a continuation from W.W.1. But he thought the invasion of Poland by Nazi Germany in 1939 actually started it.

I got so sleepy. All I understood so far was that we were going home, and maybe I'll get to see my real daddy and my new baby sister.

Ted was worried and really upset and said some bad words because the Japanese were very bad people. They had bombed us and might bomb us again before we get home. They were angry with us because we were helping England. I didn't know England or Britain.

When I woke up, our little Willis had stopped. Mom was standing at the front of it, and Ted was in the drivers seat, honking the horn and yelling, "Get in the damn car!"

"Come on Peggy, get out of the car! Mom yelled. Ted sat there with a quart of beer in a brown paper bag. "We are not going anywhere with you drinking beer in the car!" Julian yelled back.

I looked around to see if anyone was looking. We were at a gas station and a store. No one was around. I was relieved but at a second glance, I saw a couple of big boys sitting at the side of the building. One was in overalls, the other in cutoffs. They were drinking beer and smoking cigarettes, watching us with grins on their faces. They stuck their middle finger up at me and said, "F.K you." I didn't know what that meant, but I saw my cousin Howe do that to his brothers. I just put my head down and pretended not to see. I wanted to ask Mom but now wasn't the time.

Ted just sat in the car, swigging on his bottle. Not until his smelly beer was gone did we leave. I could tell that Ted was drunk by the plastered, passive, sick looking simile on his face.

That is what he looked like every time he got drunk. Mom was just relieved that he didn't buy another bottle.

Julian only had two emotions that were really hers and not theatrical: happy or angry. When she was happy, she expressed herself as a jovial sanguine. When she was angry, she could become very violent. Only under desperate self-control did she not fly into a violent rage and do something to release her anger.

At this situation, this moment, she was angry and many miles from home and her protecting sisters.

She was pregnant and in her mind was reliving an experience that she endured with James. The world's thorny switch was at her back, and she believed she deserved it for compromising and backsliding from her Lord. She was very quiet; Mom was seldom quiet except deliberate for effects. This was eerie and scary.

Ted started in. "You are becoming just like my mother. She got religion and chased my dad off and you are going to do the same thing with me. This is my vacation, for Christ sake. If a man can't have a beer once in awhile without being nagged, he is a poor excuse of a man. I will do as I damn well please, and if you don't like it, too bad."

Mom never said a word. And after some time, Ted sort of apologized and started talking in a very concerned manner about Pearl Harbor and what might happen.

Our world was never the same again. We "kids" even had a new game called Army, and we fought the Germans and the Japs right along with the American soldiers in our imaginary world.

Soon the Blue Star Service Banner was in most windows, displaying that they had loved ones in the military. It didn't matter what size the Banner was as long as it was in proportion to the size of the U.S. Flag. Each blue star represented one Service person. A banner could have up to five stars, signifying that five members were in active duty. If there were more than five members serving, another Banner would be started.

If one had been killed, there would be a gold star smaller than the blue that was placed on top so that the blue formed a border. When we kids walked by a window that had the Blue Star Banner, we faced the window and saluted.

We collected everything that could be recycled for the war effort. We had contests for the largest tin foil balls, mostly made out of chewing gum wrappers.

We were in a global war that involved all the great powers of the world. The major Allies: USSR– Joseph Stalin, USA– Franklin D. Roosevelt, UK– Winston Churchill and China– Chiang Kai-shek and the major Axis: Germany– Adolf Hitler, Japan– Hirohito, and

Italy– Benito Mussolini. This was the most widespread war in history.

Besides World War11, Los Angeles was at war with the Zoot Suitors. There were terrible riots that received as much press as the global war.

The conflict was between American servicemen stationed in Southern California and Mexican American youths, who wore Zoot Suits: a long jacket with baggy pegged pants, a long watch chain, and shoes with thick soles.

These outfits were considered unpatriotic during wartime.

The rationing of fabric was required, including for the manufacture of men's suits and all clothing that contained wool. Any wide-cut zoot suits and full women's skirts or dresses were forbidden. A network of bootleg tailors based in Los Angeles continued to produce the garments.

CHAPTER THIRTEEN

Something terrible, something sad I wish I could tell my Dad. I feel discomfort and distress; everything is in a mess. I seek for solace I never got because Ted had a thought all prepared and ready that everyone bought.

I believe that Satan himself sometimes holds the world's thorny switch, but most of the times it is one of his demons that enjoy switching us over and over again. It hurts and sometimes makes us bleed, and sometimes the thorns prick at our heart. But neither Satan nor the demon can enter in and posses a Christian's heart.

School days and friends to play with got me through the days, but the evenings and weekends were harder. I did not trust

Ted and became withdrawn in his presence. Mom did not seem to notice other than she would often tell me to get that unhappy look off my face.

Ted made my life miserable. He would whisper that he loved me and treat me as though we had a special secret from Mom.

I was no longer a happy, over talkative little girl. Instead I became distrustful, uptight and preoccupied with a burden and how to live with it.

Mom had two of her brothers in the military, and Grandma displayed two blue stars on her banner. Neither was drafted; both joined before war was declared.

John, a younger brother but not the youngest, looked like Mom's twin. The youngest, Fred, was tall and husky set for his age joined the Army when he was just thirteen, he lied about his age, and he was enlisted.

When war broke out, Grandma wrote a letter to the Military headquarters in Los

Angeles telling them what Fred had done, thinking they would discharge him because he was too young, they didn't. He had been serving in the Army for quite some time, so they did let him take leave.

Fred was home on leave in 1941 and was staying with Aunt Virginia. She loved her brothers, but especially this one; he was the baby of the family.

Not too long after his leave, Pauline started having pain in her vaginal area and was urinating frequently with pain. Virginia took her to the doctor, and he diagnosed her to have Gonorrhea. IMPOSSIBLE, she was only ten years old and never touched. She was never out of her parents' sight, and she for sure had not been penetrated nor did she have a story to tell.

It is possible to get Gonorrhea from a toilet seat. It can be transmitted through bodily fluid. The disease-causing organisms can survive for only a short time on the surface of a toilet seat, and for an infection to occur, the germs would have to be transferred from the toilet seat to the genital tract through a cut or sore on the buttocks or thighs, which is possible but very unlikely (Gonorrhea Search WebMD)

Everyone in the family, to include friends that had been in Paul and Virginia's home during the time that Pauline could have contacted the disease, had to be tested.

OH WHAT AN UPROAR

Virginia and Paul were going to kill who ever it was that had the disease and used their toilet. They ranted and raved.

The doctors told them that more than likely, Pauline was waiting outside the door anxious to urinated, as soon as the person was finished, she hopped on the toilet. He said that the bacteria can only survive on a toilet seat for seconds, and that is why it was almost impossible to contact Gonorrhea from a toilet seat but not impossible and that is how she contacted the disease.

The night before it was our turn to be checked. Mom and Ted, Virginia and Paul, Caroline and Ralph were together talking about the whole ordeal and the testing. I was seven years old now, and was listening to their excited and concerned conversation, and thought; *when they check me they will know that Ted rubbed my pee, pee*. I got so scarred. *What should I do?* I am going to tell Mama first, before the doctor does.

"Mama, come here. I need to tell you something. Come in here and I will tell you."

When I told her, she never said a word. She became stiff and turned from me. She walked back into the kitchen. I followed her. She opened a drawer, pulled out a butcher knife, and pointed it to Ted. She raised her arm and lunged it, but Caroline caught her arm before it entered into him. Caroline took the knife from Mom. Everyone was staring.

Mom cursed Ted, told him that she was going to turn him in. He said, "Don't be ridiculous, I have never touched her. Take her to the doctor and have her examined."

With the rest of the family, I was tested for gonorrhea the next morning and the tests proved that no one had it. Finally they got the report from the Military that Fred's test came back positive.

Paul and Virginia never forgave him, and he was never allowed in their home again.

Ted insisted that I be examined. They took me to the Children's hospital to be examined with an evaluation of what I claimed. Ted already knew that my hymen was not disturbed and there would be no evidence. Nothing to suggest that he was guilty of such a thing. I remember the doctor asking me questions. I remember being afraid of him and not responding. I just stared at him. I think he thought I was stupid. The doctor reported that there were no signs that I had been violated. He suggested that I might be imagining for attention or that I dreamt this occurrence.

Julian was uncertain but wanted Ted to be innocent. Everyone in the family knew the situation. My moms sister Sadie and husband Merle didn't live in the same neighborhood but lived only four miles away and they came and comforted her, reassuring her that Ted could never do anything like that.

Ted won, and he knew that there was nothing I could do about it, I wasn't smart enough to set a trap for him and I wanted everything to be okay anyway. I wanted my mommy to be happy and not be angry at me.

My mother never left the issue alone. It was continually on her mind as she constantly brought it up to Ted or her sisters and brothers. She knew down deep I was telling the truth. I think she felt guilty for not taking a stand for me. I was simply ignored about it and life went on. I didn't tell Mom about

Archie for many years. He never bothered me again. He was afraid I would tell, and I would have.

I learned after I was married and had my own children that one of my uncle's girls accused Archie. He denied it and got away with it; she was older, and they didn't want everybody to know about it. If I had known I would have come to her rescue.

I believe that all my uncles were warned to be careful around me, not to be alone with me because I had a big imagination. Except for one of my mom's brothers, they were never mean to me; they just stayed at a distance. Her one brother John, did get me alone twice to tell me I was a spoiled brat that told dirty lies about Ted, and should be ashamed of my self. Another one of her brothers loved me and always told me how much God loved me and I loved him so much.

Time never took care of the situation. Mom became the victim and always had the story to tell, always wanting to hear that Ted could never do anything like that. Those she told would look at me strangely and I would pretend I was too stupid to notice.

Mom started switching me almost everyday. She would get so angry at me. I know I irritated her by telling her everything I did and I told her again and again what Ted was doing to me but she didn't want to believe it. I think she thought she could switch it all away.

She put stripes on me with an apricot or peach limbs. She would whip be until I cried and then she would whip me until I shut up. Sometimes I think she would feel guilty because she would say that she whipped me because I needed it and she didn't want me to grow up like my Aunt Betsy. Betsy was my father's sister; an alcoholic and my mother despised her.

Every now and then Ted would come after me. He never raped me it was more like he fantasied. He would grab me, tell me he loved me and try to kiss me, hold me and fondle me.

I would scream at him, kick him, and tell him I was going to tell Mom. He just laughed, released me and went about his business as if nothing happened. And when he got a chance, he would do it again.

CHAPTER FOURTEEN

A nightmare is what I called it, but it was real, I saw it. The ambulance came, she was in pain, and nothing would ever be the same.

My baby brother was born Theodore Glenn Tucker, he is a beautiful baby with curly reddish blond hair and big blue eyes.

I smothered him like he was my own baby. I love him so much; I dressed him, changed him, took care of him, and walked him in his buggy. And he was my solace.

Teddy was just a couple months old when he became fussy and crying like something was wrong. He didn't have a fever, and Mom thought he might have a little colic. After a couple of days a fever was present, and she decided he needed to go to the doctor. She would take him when Ted got home from work at 4:30 P.M.; we didn't have a phone in those days.

That evening, Ted did not come home after work, and Mom was really up set because she was unable to get a hold of him. We went ahead and had dinner. She was quiet, so I tried to talk to her and said, "I wish he wouldn't drink" She said, "So do I, Peggy, He would be a good husband if he didn't. You need to be careful, that when you grow up, you don't make the mistake of marring a man that drinks".

Teddy Glenn had been fussy and feverish all day and we couldn't comfort him. Mom asked me to skate over to aunt Virginia's and tell her that Ted is not home, that the baby has a high fever, and needs to go to the doctor.

Teddy had a double mastoid infection. The doctor said that he had an infection of the sinus behind the middle ear, and it was very serious. They admitted him in the Children's Hospital immediately. He was a very sick baby.

Virginia drove Mom home to tell Ted. He wasn't home yet. They waited, and were having a cup of coffee when he drove into the driveway.

Ted was in a drunken stupor. My mother started beating him with her fist. She pushed him into the bathtub and turned the cold water on him; there was no shower in the bathroom. He never fought back; he just had that stupid, silly plastered smile on his face. Julian became very theatrical to get his attention, to snap him out of it. She screamed, "Your baby is in the hospital dying."

Aunt Virginia took Mom back to the hospital, where she stayed with her baby. And I stayed with Aunt Virginia, Uncle Paul, and my cousins Pauline, and Marylou. Marylou had lived with them since my mother moved out with Ted. They just lived a few streets apart, and the girls went to the same school together.

Caroline, Marylou's mother didn't think it looked right or that it was right for Marylou to be home alone with three older brothers and Ralph being there sometime because he never had a steady job.

While I stayed there I was able to continue going to school if I skated. It was much to far to walk. Miss Anderson, our principal, gave special permission to bring my skates to school knowing the circumstances; I was there two weeks.

I cried and worried for my baby brother everyday. Aunt Virginia would give me an update, letting me know he was going to be okay.

Teddy Glenn came home, I came home and Ted promised that he would never stop after work for a drink again. And he didn't... for a couple of months.

Teddy Glen was about five months old. He had just started sitting up. I would prop pillows around him and play with him. He would extend his arms to me. That would make me elated and thrilled. Mom encouraged it, and trusted me to watch Teddy while they went to the store or whatever. I taught him to play peek-a-boo, and I talked to him like he understood everything I said. He for sure was my solace.

The next time Ted came home drunk was a living nightmare. Julian went crazy, she went into the bathroom, and took from the medicine cabinet a two-ounce bottle of iodine and drank it straight down. I knew what it was because we used it for an anesthetic in those days. Iodine was used for everything, when I had a sore throat, Mom would mix iodine and glistering together to swab it.

Oh I screamed, "No mama, no." I screamed for Ted to do something. He just sat on the couch with a stupid smile plastered on his face.

I ran outside and I started screaming to the neighbors, and pounding the sidewalk, "My Mommy drank iodine! My Mommy is dead! My Mommy is dead!"

Someone with a phone must have heard because the ambulance and the police came. They talked to Ted, and by then he was more responsive.

I assume he followed the ambulance to the hospital. I was left alone with Teddy Glenn, but soon Aunt Caroline came for us.

Julian knew Ted was too drunk to know what she was doing or even care. How could she do that? Who would take care of Teddy Glenn? She wanted to die, but who would take care of my baby brother?

I think my mother really felt trapped, She couldn't drive and she had never been employed. She didn't think she could make it on her own, and she wanted out.

ALL SWEPT UNDER THE RUG

My mother was intelligent. She could add columns up quickly in her head, and she would sometimes demonstrate that to me for fun. She would have been an asset to any type of business.

They just kept her over night in the hospital. I don't know what she went through there, but she could not talk for at least two days, and she was really hoarse and gravely for a couple of weeks. Ted said that her esophagus was burned and blistered from the iodine, and that she was crazy and would do anything to have her own way.

That was not true. The world's thorny switch had been on this lady for the last ten years. Her first husband James was a womanizer and an alcoholic and Mom went through hell with him. Her second husband was an alcoholic, molesting her child, and she had to fight with him every morning to get up, and go to work. She lost a full-term baby girl, and she was beside herself. Maybe today they would have diagnosed her with having a mental break down. She truly was a victim.

It was common for women to feel helpless in her day and even more so before her day, especially if they came from large families that believed that females were to become homemakers. She was born in 1915 five years before women could even vote. My mother was raised that way. Her parents didn't think it was necessary for girls to be educated over sixth or maybe eight grade.

Most women were so low paid that they could not support themselves let alone a family. There is much more opportunity for women today. However, women and men both have a hard time supporting a family today. Many women are still being disrespected in the work place with sexual harassment and low pay but for most families today it takes two in a household to support the family.

CHAPTER FIFTEEN

No dust in this air, the "Arkies" declare. We'll settle here with spring water so clear. The water is pure, and the Hondo River is near. We'll buy us a lot and live on the plot.

*M*om's brother, Allen was telling Ted that there was property for sale just eight miles east of where we lived. It was in the country up in the hills selling real cheap. Ted wanted to see it, so that Saturday we drove up to where our new home would be for the next eight years.

There were three lots that had a structure on them that were for sale and several vacant lots to choose from. One lot had a small two-bedroom stucco house on it that was level to the street and even had a driveway,

Mom liked that one; but they wanted $900.00 for it. Most of the properties were on a hill with a narrow path to their shack (dumps) that they lived in.

But there was one short area on a long street running north and south where four shacks were probably twenty-five feet below the street level. And one of those dumps was for sale for only $350.00. It had no path down to it. The only way down the steep sloping hill was to slide on your butt or slide down on a flat cardboard. Yes, you guessed it; that is the one Ted bought.

The neighbors on the north side had a 50' long descending dirt driveway to get to their shack. The people on the south side framed in fill dirt to create a flatter area and framed a descending cement staircase of probably 12 to 15 steps down.

Our coop may have been 800 square feet, and as all the coops, we had water, gas and electricity. There were three rooms: a kitchen that was plastered, A living room with button board walls waiting to be plastered, a bed room with button board waiting to be plastered and a walk in closet just framed.

Our coop sat on a lot 100 x 200 feet in size. There was a shed, an outhouse, an incinerator, and a fairly emptied cesspool covered with some boards on the back portion that stunk.

The south side had a four-foot picket fence and the back or west side was fenced with barbed wire and caster bean plants. The North side was not fenced, which was a good thing because we would have never been able to move our furniture in without the use of our neighbor's driveway.

In our yard we had three peach trees, two apricot trees, a pomegranate tree, and wild blackberries scattered around in several areas.

Before move-in day, Mom and her three sisters cleaned the coop, including the outhouse.

BEVERLY MCCOY (HARLOW)

When Ted asked the neighbors if we could use their driveway to move in, to his surprise they weren't too friendly about it but agreed to it. They let him know right up front that we wouldn't be welcome to use their driveway for the entrance to our shack in general. We needed our own entryway to our property immediately and that didn't look possible.

I was helping by staying out of the sisters' way and exploring around our lot. I was worried about the outhouse because I was afraid of spiders and thought they were in there.

The woodshed looked old and dilapidated. It 's foundation was not level, and the whole shed looked like it was tilting. It was probably 12 x 14 feet or thereabouts. The wooden door had no lock. I had a funny feeling standing before it. I wanted to open the door and look inside, but I thought, *what if there are big spiders in their and one would jump on me?*

I am not a sissy girl; I was going to open it. I would just pull the door open and run. As I reached for the knob, I pulled. It opened just a little bit, I started to pull again when the door burst open and a kid ran out, pushing me as he ran away.

I watched him scramble through the neighbors yard. He had a pole sticking out of his pant leg and no foot. He had one leg with a bare foot and a pole for the other leg. I had never seen anything like that before. Who was he and why was he in the shed?

Instead of going into the shed, I ran to tell Mama what happened. She and her sisters all came out to see but did not believe me, and Aunt Sadie said that it sounded like a pretty wild story to her, and that I had a big imagination. Ted loved hearing that. He said that I probably had seen a pirate with a peg leg at the movies, and that is where I got the idea.

Ted acted a little rejected and even a little worried after talking to the neighbor about the driveway. He just stood in front of the steep incline, speculating what we could do for a quick temporary entrance. There was none. He realized that other than a sealed lid for the cesspool, an entrance path would be his first project.

I think the neighbors on the north side of us originally owned our property, and used the one driveway for the four coops, and sold this one to Ted without the rights of the driveway and thought it to be funny. While Ted drew a plan, and started digging, and shaping an entrance way we slid down the hill. I thought it was fun until it rained. Red mud is very slippery when it gets wet.

I looked inside the shed again. I wasn't afraid this time. Mom and her sisters looked in there to see if there was any evidence that someone had been hiding, and they saw nothing, and I got a good peek too.

There was nothing surprising in there, just some old wood pieces, and barbwire on the floor, and a broken up dresser. Ted would use all this junk in his fill dirt for the patio.

Under a piece of the wood I saw a dark blue snow hat covered in lint, and a rolled-up knitted blue rag. I didn't want to touch them. They looked dirty. But I was curious and got a stick, pulled them out, and picked them up with the stick, the blue rag was a sweater. I showed Mom. She said that they were just junk that was left by the people that used to live here, go throw them into the incinerator; I did.

I thought about the boy that I saw run out of there, and wondered if that hat and sweater was his. No body believed I saw a boy, they just think I imagine things. My mother looked puzzled at what to do about it. If I was lying, she needed to whip me. I stuck with my story. She said that if she found out I was lying, she needed to whip me hard. Then she let it go. She must have had a feeling that I was telling the truth because she never let anything go.

CHAPTER SIXTEEN

"As cheap as dirt" is what they used to say, but dirt is not cheap today. In the hills of red clay where I grew up, it now cost a million to buy lot with a house and a pot.

It seemed like Ted and Mom dug red clay, moved it, and made the decline less steep with fill dirt for a thousand years. It didn't take that long, but it did take over three months working just on the weekends and in the evening. Their goal, of course, was to complete it before winter set in. They prayed to have it completed by October. They framed steps and a short retaining wall on each side of the steps that would be cement.

Ted and Mom looked for junk, which wasn't easy to find because everything that could be recycled went to the war effort. They used junk with fill dirt to construct a patio at least 8 by12 feet, and three feet deep with the cement surface three inches thick. There were three steps extending from the patio to the ground all was cemented.

Ted really did well with this project. He and Mom did most of the work on the weekends, and I took care of Teddy Glenn. Ted even seemed anxious to work on it in the evening after dinner. He was so tired at night that he went to bed early, and was able to get up the next morning for work.

I think the CCC Camp taught him a lot about moving dirt. He seemed to know what he was doing and enjoyed doing it. He really enjoyed drawing the plans. The hardest part for Ted was the framing. He didn't know a saw from a hammer (quoting the cliché)

Cement work is an art and a good trade, Ted and my mother didn't seem to realize that. They mixed their own cement in a little electric powered cement mixer using a fifty-foot power cord plugged in at the coop. They poured it themselves a little bit at a time. We had the best-looking entrance to the property of the four houses. The fourth house belonged to the same owner of the long driveway and they just used their long dirt driveway for both houses.

What was better about their property was that you could drive a car down to it even though it was steep. There was no way to have a driveway for us or for the neighbor's on the south side of our property.

We hardly had a place to park. Actually our parking was probably no wider than ten feet and maybe sixty feet long. There was enough room for three cars to get off the street. It seemed scary to park along the side of a cliff; not a good idea in fog.

It was summer, and Mom let me explore the neighborhood during the weekdays. All I had to do was cross the street and hike up a twenty-foot hill. At the top of that hill, as far as I could see, were rolling hills covered with sweet-smelling green grass and California poppies popping out here and there. The sight was incredibly beautiful, with ravines that were in some places fifty or maybe seventy-five feet deep. The whole scene was breathtaking.

I could play up there alone for hours, sometimes with a stray dog and soon with my three cousins Bobby, Larry, and Jimmy. What an army game we would play. My biggest challenge was to get on the other side of a ravine. Jumping across when it was narrow enough, hiking down, and hiking up the other side when too wide. Today that whole area has been turned into a residential suburb of tract homes-expensive ones too.

There was so much to explore in my hills. Every weekday, after chores I would go another way then the day before.

Each coop that I saw, during my exploring, was a different size and shape. A few looked slanted, and most were small, sitting on large, uneven lots. One or two looked as though they where about to collapse. I could see a few two-story houses in the distance higher up in the hills.

It would take me a long time to explore this neighborhood. There were no sidewalks for roller-skating and there was so much to see and so many kids to say hi to. No body asked me who I was. They just stared and said, "Hi".

Most everyone raised chickens and rabbits, and had big gardens. Their chicken coops were not designed too differently from the coop they lived in. No one had pigs or cows. There must have been some code against that kind of farm animal; otherwise pigs and cows would have been there.

Not too far and on the same street that I lived was a little mom and pop store called

Tinker's and on the seemingly same paved lot sat a church with a cross on top. Both shared the extra pavement for parking. They were on a cross street. Right headed up to higher hills and more residents. Left wound down out of the hills.

I turned left, and for at least three blocks on my right was a stream of water flowing maybe a foot or so from the paved street. It came out of the hills from the Honda River and ended to a small shallow pond with tadpoles, frogs or horny toads. A mound of rocks separates the deeper part of the pond.

The whole area was landscaped with cypresses, weeping willows, wild blackberries and much foliage to hide in.

This became my special place, a place to hide and maybe live. I could sleep under a tree by a big rock. I could bring my own blanket, and I could eat blackberries. I would sneak home now and then, not letting anyone see me, and maybe get some bread. Take a peek at Teddy Glenn and Mom to see if they missed me and see if they are okay.

A little ways from the pond was a cross street. To the left you could see the beginning of the sidewalks that led to the school that I will be attending in September. If I move to my pond, I could sneak to school before the kids got there and before anyone could see me. I would get my books, paper, and pencils and hide in the attic above my classroom and listen to the teacher so I wouldn't get behind. No one would know, and Marylou and Pauline could not call me dumb because I would still be almost as smart as they were.

No one would ever be able to find me at my pond. I would have dogs and make a garden where no one could see it, and I would play with pollywogs and my dogs' everyday.

I could skate to the stores, sneak into them without them seeing me, and hide until the store closed. And after everyone was gone, I would put some new cloths and new shoes on.

I might get a boys jacket to keep me warm at night, and maybe even get a boys two wheel-bike, and sneak it back to my pond.

I would have everything I needed, and that Ted Tucker would be sorry that he hadn't told the truth. I felt real sorry for myself and thought, *what would happen if they found the bike and the clothes? They'd put me in jail. No one would come for me because they would be too ashamed of me. God wouldn't help me because I was a thief.* I cried.

Soon I forgot about all of that and made little houses out of the wet reddish sand clay and noticed that the sun was going down.

I took off running for home. I didn't know the way home from the school, so I went home the way I got to the pond and that was the longer way home.

I knew I was late and in trouble. Being in trouble meant that I would get a whipping with a peach tree switch. I knew I was suppose to be home in time to take the clothes off the line and fold them, set the table, and maybe make a salad before Ted got home from work I had no excuse.

Mom was worried and furious with me when I got home. Not only did I get a whipping after dinner, but she also told me that if she couldn't trust me to be home in time, I was too young to explore the neighborhood.

I cried, and begged her to give me one more chance. I don't know where she got it, but she brought out a watch and said, "You can't go any place tomorrow, but I will let you explore around the neighborhood the day after tomorrow because you have been doing such a good job taking care of Teddy Glenn for us on the weekends. You are to be home by 3:00 p.m. and she showed me on the watch that the big hand was on the twelve and the little hand was on the three.

I could wear it so I would always know what time it was. Three p.m. was the dead line. I was to wear the watch only when she gave permission to leave the yard and go skating or exploring.

I thought I was the luckiest girl in the world. Mom and Ted taught me how to tell time that night. The next day I practiced, verbally and recited counting by fives and tens most of the day: five minutes after, ten minute to and etc., driving my poor mother crazy.

Thursday after chores, I left home and toured in another direction. I turned right, walked a block, turned right, and crossed the street. This brought me to a different entrance to the same school that I would be attending in September. The street by the pond took me to the side of the school and this street took me to the front of it.

This area was out of our hills and was considered to be in the city. The people here did not want any part of those "Arkies" who lived in the hills. The hills were an unincorporated community. Most of the residents that lived there migrated from Arkansas during the third wave of the Dust Bowl in 1939-40.

This area in the city would be my skating area, and it was only a couple of blocks from where I lived. I could skate everywhere in this city and to a large grocery store for Mom that wasn't much more than a mile away. I could skate to the movies, a Currie's ice cream store, and to a Thrifty drug store.

Most of the streets were either downhill or up hill but the closer I got to the main Boulevard the more level they became. Every street had sidewalks. And I don't think there was a coop in the area. There were only beautiful homes, all sitting on 100 x 100-foot lots or much larger with garages, and cemented driveways, and beautiful lawns. It was a beautiful neighborhood for mostly the well-established blue-collar workers. Oh, there were the white-collar area too, but not in my skating range.

CHAPTER SEVENTEEN

Ted's secret plan is why he bought the coop and land. There will be no more rent, and the utilities are just a small dent. It's not so much; it's not a bunch.

*T*ed's unceasing thoughts with ideas of how to quit his routine life and boring job finally were satisfied by the decision to go into the concession business and be an independent entrepreneur. His father knew Mr. Jacob Muller, who was the main distributor for supplies, machines, and tips on sport events, carnivals, rodeos and what ever that was coming up.

Ralph, meanwhile, worked for the racetracks or the coliseum and never wanted to do more than that, as he was a retired tailor and just wanted to work enough to get by. He found an even better way to "get by" with Caroline, if he could just get rid of her kids oh how happy he would be. He was having too many physical accidents and he thought they were all set-up by Caroline's kids.

Ralph was convincing Ted that there was a lot of money to be made in the concession business if you became independent. Depending on the size of the business, you paid twenty-five to forty percent of what you sold to the company or owner of the event, and the rest minus overhead was yours.

Popcorn was a novelty in those days. They sold it in the movie houses and the ballparks, but it wasn't plentiful like it is today, and there was no microwave ovens to compete with them.

Ted didn't quit his job at Lockheed right away because he needed to be sure of a paycheck to complete some necessary work on the coop– a bathroom next. The bathroom would have been first if we had had some way to get down to our coop, but we didn't.

First Ted needed to convince my mother that going into the concession business was what they should do. They could work together, and make more money and have more freedom to enjoy life. They could even take Teddy Glenn and me to the events that they worked; they wouldn't need a sitter.

Ted would need to trade the Willis in for a van, so as to haul the equipment and stock. He needed at least two Popcorn machines and a generator. He had a goal, and he aimed to achieve it.

The summer went by fast. The entrance to our coop was almost finished but not before I started to school. It was a difficult six more weeks before we could use the entryway.

When the project started taking shape and anyone could see what we were doing, Mom started walking up and down the neighbor's driveway holding Teddy Glenn in her arms with a defiant posture that said, *Just try and stop me.* In fact, when the family or friends came to visit, which was often, they walked down and up that driveway not realizing they were intruding on the neighbors. There was no other way down except to slide. Mom and Ted never told visitors that the neighbors said that we couldn't use their driveway.

When I started school, I used the driveway too or else I would ruin my new school clothes. My mother bought me two new dresses and two blouses. Aunt Virginia gave me three beautiful skirts, two pullover sweaters, and a coat, that Pauline had outgrown. But they were beautiful, just like new, and they fit me perfect. I was proud of my clothes, except for my shoes. The souls were still attached to my shoes and Mom said they would do for a while. They always bought me those ugly brown oxfords anyway.

I was one of the first to arrive at school. "Miss Dotson" was written on the blackboard.

I had not met anyone to play with all summer. I was anxious and excited, as everyone is on the first day back to school. I was confident with my pretty new dress and long curls that Mom twisted on her finger.

I was determined that I wouldn't smile when the teacher called out my name. Everyone would turn to look at me, and I didn't want to look excited. I would just hold my mouth real stiff and say, "Here". It never turns out that way though. When the teacher calls out my name, my lips always spread clear across my face no matter how hard I try to be stiff.

There were so many desks to choose from. In fact, there were forty, and all but two were filled before the bell rang. Those two would be filled, but there was two absent on the first day.

I breathed in with almost an audible squeal from my voice when the boy that burst out of our shed walked through the door. After the bell, Miss Dotson took roll and arranged us in alphabetic order to help her memorize our name; of course that wouldn't have been necessary for me. She would have memorized my name after the third day.

There was already a leader in our class with her special girl friends. This would be her forth year, counting kindergarten, in this school, and she couldn't wait to let me know I wasn't welcome. Her name was Dorothy the Dot.

She was the leader because she was extraordinarily bright. She was always miss sunshine. Her parents were the pillars of the community, and she was the teacher's helper.

When the war broke out, thousands of positions were abandoned in order to fill the Military's needs and demands. Thousands of teachers, men and women, abandoned their teaching positions to fill the vacancies for higher-paying positions. Many teachers joined the military, and many took jobs in wartime industries and even government organizations. There was a severe teacher shortage in every state. Classes became over crowded with as many as forty or more kids in a classroom.

When the war was over, the problem continued because a high percentage of college students dropped out of teacher training programs because they didn't want to spend four years and tuition on a profession with such low pay. Teachers received lower pay than any professional group. In order to fill the thousands of teaching positions, schools hired men and women who did not meet the requirements for a teacher's license.

---❋---

I kept looking at the boy who had run out of our shed. His desk was to the left and two ahead of me. His name was Dale Fadner.

When Miss Dotson called his name, he said, "Here" and laid his head down on his desk, extending both arms forward.

His straight blond hair was not combed, his colored shirt was halfway tucked into his genes, and the peg in his belt to hold his pants up was in the last hole. He had a black and white ankle high tennis shoe on and I could see the pole that extended as his other leg.

"What is an "Arkie"? I asked at the dinner table. Mom and Ted both looked at me surprised and I continued, "Am I an Arkie?"

"No, said Ted, your not an "Arkie" you are a "Prune Picker," An Arkie is from Aransas, and a prune picker is from California." "I don't pick prunes," I replied. "No, but that's what they call people from California." A boy called me an "Arkie." "Well, he was wrong," said Ted.

The boy who has a pole for a leg is in my classroom. He sits by me. "Peggy, why didn't you tell us he was in your classroom the first day?" Ted asked. "I don't know. I didn't think of it".

"Did you ask him what he was doing in our shed"? No, he doesn't talk. "He doesn't talk at all?" "Not to me."

"Do you like your new school", Mom asked. "Yes, Miss. Dotson is real nice, and when we have recess, there are two bells. The first one that rings is called a silent bell. That means we are to quit talking or moving. The second bell means we are to walk back to class. It's fun because if it rings when you are on one foot, you have to stay that way without moving until the bell rings."

"I think I am going to find out why that Dale Fadner was in our shed", I thought. *I'll challenge him to a wrestling match if he won't talk, and I'll twist his arm up behind his back until he* does**.** *About six kids in my class walk home going toward my pond, and Dale was one of them. After school I'll challenge him.*

I did, and we started wrestling, the other kids were watching and yelling, "Get her, 'Peg,' before she grabs you!"

I got a hold of his arm, twisted it behind him, and started pulling it up. I yelled, "Say 'uncle'! He wouldn't so I pulled harder and yelled, "Say 'uncle'!"

He said, "I will never say it to a girl, you can break my arm, and I will never say it".

I dropped his arm when he said that and said, "You won, Dale. Do you want to do it again tomorrow?"

His eyes and forehead got real red and He said, "I am going to beat the shit out of you tomorrow." Then he ran.

Dale lived up in the hills with four brothers and a sister. We became secret friends because he didn't want anyone to see him talking to a girl. After we became friends, he always smiled at me as if he couldn't help it. His lips just stretched across his face. He didn't want to smile, and I knew exactly how he felt.

He could run on his peg leg, play kickball better then the rest of the boys. There was nothing he couldn't do that everyone else could do but wear two shoes. He wouldn't tell me why he was in our shed, but I found out one day.

It was a Saturday, and Mom said that I didn't have to watch Teddy Glenn. She gave me a penny to buy candy at Tinkers.

I wanted to explore the higher hills that I had seen from a distance. On the way, I heard some chickens clucking quite loudly, as though they were being disturbed. I walked toward them. They were flopping, running and even growling. I saw Dale and his father in their chicken coop yard.

I quickly squatted down behind a scraggly bush of some kind that was covered with bees. I didn't want Dale and his father to see me, so I stayed right where I was and held very still.

What I witnessed was horror. The drunken man was small, skinny, and absolutely wild, cussing foul words at Dale. He had a chicken by its legs, and he was whipping Dale with it. Dale was screaming, "Don't, Daddy! Stop it!"

Dale's mother was standing outside of the chicken yard crying, "Stop it, Fred, and come in the house!"

"Not until I teach this kid a thing or two!" He whipped Dale with that chicken until it was dead. Dale had chicken blood and his own blood all over him. Blood sprayed everywhere. It was gruesome.

Fred abruptly stopped whipping and started dancing, pleased with him self. He raised one leg high and then the other, screaming, "Clean this mess up! Clean it up!" Dale bolted out of the pen and started running.

I ran after him. He saw me, and rubbed his tears away. He said, "I am going to kill that son of a bitch, I am going to kill him you just watch and see."

I comforted him and asked him, "What happen?" He said, "The same thing that happens all the time. He gets drunk, comes home, grabs one of us boys, takes us to the chicken coop, and whips us with a chicken. It's usually not this bad, but he was crazy mad at me. When he came home, he was drunk and started pushing Mom, telling her a bunch of crap. I told him to leave her alone, and he went crazy."

"Dale, I have a special hiding place with a pond that has pollywogs in it. There are a lot of trees around and bushes to hide under. You could get in the pond and wash all that blood away. And I will go home and get my blanket for you and bring you a sandwich."

"Peggy, that pond is not a hiding place. Everyone goes there. They have picnics with their family, they play catch, and it's usually crowded out on the weekends. Everyone would see me."

"Oh, I have never been there on the weekend. I love that place," I said. "I have another idea, sneak to my shed. We have a hose hooked up at the back. You lay down in the tall grass by the shed, and I will hose the blood away. If anyone comes out, of the house, I'll pretend like I am playing with the hose, and you can crawl around to the back of the shed. If no one comes out you can wash all the blood away, and then you can hide in the shed. I will bring you a towel and my blanket and a sandwich."

Please, Dale. You can't stay here. Come on. I can hide you."

He said," I am going to kill that crazy drunk, I am going to kill him."

"No. If you did that, you would go to hell and burn forever and ever.

"Oh Peggy, what are you talking about? I never heard of such a thing."

Let's go Dale before your brothers find you and take you home."

"He'll sleep it off and be okay tomorrow. He'll raise hell for hours yet. My brothers will clean up the mess. Mom will want them to find me. She'll cry and he will drink vodka until he passes out. I'll sneak home tonight, so don't worry, Peggy." Dale and I were friends until the end.

CHAPTER EIGHTEEN

There were quarters and dimes I found sometimes. A dollar or a five were seldom found, but pennies were always on the ground. "Popcorn, Popcorn, get your red-hot Pop Corn" sold from my tray hooked on me to stay. A dollar a day is what I got for pay. The money I found was my secret stash; nobody knew I had so much cash.

Oh, how I hated the outhouse, and my imagination ran wild in there. Mom hated it too, and her grievances were heard loud and clear. We were city people and always had a bathroom.

Keeping clean was a real choir. Looking pretty? I don't remember a mirror. Even the Children of Israel had mirrors when Moses parted the Red Sea. We didn't have a mirror until we got our new bathroom.

We did have hot and cold running water in the kitchen, but it didn't serve well as a bathroom too. I guess we were spoiled in that I couldn't even imagine going through the clean up process without running water. So building the bathroom was next.

Drawing the plans was no problem and there were no codes to worry about. The expense caused most of the delays. The framing and plumbing was expensive, and Ted didn't know a hammer from a saw. Ted's uncle Ray helped him to build on to our coop a bathroom. It took more time to complete than Ted thought, but his secret plan to quit his job kept him excited and contented.

The bathroom consisted of a toilet, sink, and shower. The shower was cemented with a high ledge in the front of it. We could fill it up with a few inches of water and sit in it.

The walls and ceiling were first prepared with button board. That was easy. Plastering was not so easy. The salesman sold Ted all that he needed and told him it was easy-just pick up the wet plaster with the trough and spread it on.

Ted and my mother never saw a trough before or wet plaster and found that it wasn't so easy. It was different and harder then even smoothing cement for them, but the room was small, and they never gave up.

The walls and ceiling got plastered. They were not very smooth and even had a bulge here and there, but they painted them and put up a medicine cabinet with a mirror, a towel rack and two hooks on the back of the door to hang clothes. It was a real bathroom that they built themselves, and they were proud of it.

Ted's next task was to convince Julian that going into the concession business (selling popcorn, cotton candy, and snow cones) was the smart thing to do. If he could make her have a vision that they would succeed, have whatever they wanted, and have time together and be happy, she would go for it. It wasn't hard to plant the vision in Mom's head, she like the idea of having their own business and being a part of earning their income.

The first thing they did was trade the Willis off for a 1939 dark blue panel van.

Ted then cleaned out the shed for the equipment and storage, fixed it up real nice with plywood on the walls and heavy shelves for his tools, power cords, a dolly, yard tools, stock, equipment, and what ever else Mom didn't want in the coop. Ted was a very orderly and tidy man. Everything had its own place, and his storage shed was no exception. He turned that shed into a perfect storage house for their business.

They started with only two popcorn machines. With in two years, they added a couple of cotton candy machines, and a couple of snow cone machines. He bought all his machines and stock from Mr. Jacob Muller, who gave them the opportunity to bid for some really good, steady events, which they got.

Ted gave a two-week notice and quit his so-called monotones job. He and Julian were in business, and he was the happiest man on earth for a while.

We worked the wrestling matches on Wednesday evenings and the boxing matches Thursday evenings. They were steady jobs. We worked the motorcycle races, rodeos, and school carnivals and had no trouble getting events. Ted even turned some down. He was not a workaholic. He stayed cool, and that's why he did so well in the concession business.

I was nine the first time I hustled popcorn for Ted and my mother, and I though I was really special. I wore a money belt to make change, and the popcorn tray was strapped over my shoulders. It was unique to see a little girl yelling, "Popcorn! Get you're red-hot Popcorn!" I usually sold tray after tray before I got into the stands. I carried fifty small bags of corn for ten cents a bag.

In between trays or a break, maybe lunch, I would go into the crowd and look for dropped coins. I did quite well finding lost change, much better then my pay, and I became very popular with the neighborhood kids in the hills at Tinkers mom and pop store. Mom never did find out about all that cash I carried around.

My new friend, Lillian Anderson from class, lived real close to the Fadner's. You could see the back of their hill from her house. Mom let me walk home with her after school, and we stopped at Tinkers for an orange soda that I paid for from my stash of cash.

I liked Lillian, she was a very large girl-not fat, just much taller and bigger than me. She had hair that grew about an inch passed her hair line all across her forehead. She would try to shave it off because the kids would tease her and call her a monkey.

Lillian had three older sisters, and their names all started with an *L.* They lived in a two-bedroom coop with a bathroom, a driveway, and a garage. All tilted a little.

The Father was a merchant marine and seldom, if ever, home. Her Mother had a very bad reputation, and the rumors about her were ghastly. My mother didn't know anything about the rumors of the different men being there at all hours, so she let me play in Lillian's house.

We were cutting out paper dolls on her front steps one time, and she said," Do you know how Dale lost his leg?" "No, he didn't tell me."

"See that hill?" She pointed to the back of his property. The hill extending down must have been an incline of twenty-five feet, an easy climb up or down. The way it was slanted was something like our neighbors drive way but steeper.

Lillian continued, "My mother told me that Dale was only four years old, and his brother was pushing him in their wheelbarrow, but not by the handle grips. They were too high for him to reach. He was pushing the wheelbarrow and pushed it over the edge of that hill by accident." She pointed to the hill again.

"The wheel barrel rolled and toppled over. Dale tumbled down the hill and landed into some broken-up cement. His leg was almost severed, his arm was broken, and his face was all bloody. The ambulance came. Everyone thought he was dead because he didn't cry or move."

The story made me cry, and I wondered if I twisted the arm that he had broken.

Lillian went on. "My mother said that they couldn't save his leg they cut it off below the knee, and his arm was in a cast for a long time. That night Mr. Fadner went to the edge of that hill and started screaming real loud. My mother said that she thought he had Indian in him."

"I have to go home Lil," I'll see you at school tomorrow." I cried all the way home and asked God to give him back his leg and never let his arm hurt again.

I also wondered how you could have Indian in you. What did Lillian mean? I know what an Indian is and Mr. Fadner doesn't look like an Indian.

Lillian came to my house to walk with me to school. It was the long way for her. She was excited and said several families are going to the pond Saturday. She wondered if we could go?

"I don't know, "I said. "My parents usually work on Saturday, but I'll ask, Mom, Lillian is here. We're leaving for school. Some of our neighbors are going to the pond Saturday, and Lillian has invited us to go".

"We'll be working Saturday, but it is an early cat show, so we might be home early enough to come in the afternoon. But Peggy, you can go by yourself. We won't need you, and we'll be home early."

"Oh, Mrs. Grabs, thank you", squealed Lillian". "Her name isn't Mrs. Grabs; it is Mrs. "Tucker," I said. My real dad's name is Grabs, and that is why my name is Grabs. Mom, can I bring my own picnic bag and wear my bathing suit under my slacks in case it is warm enough to go swimming? I don't know, '*can*' you? Replied my mom. "You'd better get going or you're going to be late for school."

I didn't think Saturday would ever get here. I wish I could bring fried chicken and potato salad. Mom didn't have time. She told me to make my self a baloney sandwich and take some cookies and an orange. I took enough for Dale in case he came.

As soon as they left, I put my watch on, it was 7:30 a.m., and I was on my way to the pond. I imagined all the things I was going to do. But when I arrived, there was no one there and I panicked.

It was barely light and so quiet that it was easy to hear the birds and different sounds that you don't hear when people are present. This was still my special place.

I sat by the pond, looking for the tadpoles a minute or two, and thought, *maybe no one would come, and maybe Lillian was just imagining a great picnic. "No one else said anything about it. Boy, I'll beat her (ass-K-me-no-questions, Ill tell you no lie) if she tricked me.*

There was no one there, but I noticed three old doors. One door was sitting on two horse saws, and two were propped up against a willow tree. There were two big round tubs sitting on the ground and two rock rings for weenies or marshmallows, the same kind we used at the beach.

I heard someone coming and I ran behind some foliage to hide. I saw three men coming with six planks, nails, and a couple of hammers. They hammered the boards together and placed the doors on them.

And then they brought two big blocks of ice and placed them on flat cardboard. Using an ice pick, they chipped down the middle of each until they broke in half. Then they placed them in the buckets and finished chipping. They brought twigs and wood for the fire rings.

The men left, it seemed like a long time before anyone else came. I looked at my watch. It was 10:05 a.m. I had to go to the bathroom, but there was no place to go.

The men came back with more ice and wood. They carried in a couple of boxes of soft drinks and beer, loaded the tubs, and covered them with more ice.

Soon people were carrying in their own chairs, tablecloths, boxes packed with their own dishes, silverware, and food to share. The women laid out the table clothes on the doors that became perfect tables as though they did it every week. They seemed to just know what came first and what to do.

They brought fried rabbit, fried chicken, and also weenies and marsh mellows for the kids to hold over the fire rings.

They brought potato salad, Cole slaw, lettuce, pasta salad, baked beans, and canned corn. They also had more ice blocks to be broken up as the chips melted away.

We played kickball first, and I thought I was going to pee my pants. I asked Lillian where the bathroom was, and she asked, "Number one or number two?"

I said, "both". "You have to go home for number two for number one just go hide somewhere and go. You can come to my house it's closer. Come on; I'll go with you."

"No, I better go home, I don't think it's farther anyway."

"Why can't you just hide in those trees over there and go? Asked Lillian. "I'll find some paper from one of the boxes, and I will watch out for you."

"Do you promise you won't leave until I am through?

"I promise but only if you hurry". If you ever tell anyone Lil I won't be your friend, and I'll beat you up." "I won't tell. Go on so we can play."

We played all day. Hide and Seek, Capture the Flag, ball, in and out of the water. What was best is that my problems were set-aside for all of that day. I felt I was accepted as part of their group. I was not a stranger.

These people knew how to play. They brought banjos and fiddles to sing and dance to folk songs about their farms and journey to California. It was so much fun, I was never going to tell them I was a prune picker, I wanted to be an Arkie just like them.

I put my cookies and my oranges on the table, but I hid the baloney sandwiches. It seemed so unappetizing compared to what everyone else brought. Four kids from my class were there. There would be five if Dale showed up. There were several kids and babies.

Lillian sisters were older and nice to me. They told me that everyone would stand and pray before they filled their plate, and then you could help yourself for anything you wanted all day long. Dale, his brothers, and his Mother came and brought food. No one would want an old baloney sandwich, and I convinced my self that it was smart to hide my sandwiches so no one would make fun.

CHAPTER NINTEEN

"It's almost three o'clock, I thought. I had to be home by three or *Mama* would switch me. I said my good byes and wondered why Mama and Ted didn't come. *Maybe I should wait the picnic is so great. If they come we will have more fun. Teddy Glen would extend his arms out for me. And I would be proud and happy as could be.*

I started to leave when I saw Mom and Ted coming. I was elated and started waving my arms for them to see where we were. They smiled, and I took Teddy Glen, I was so proud of him. The day was still young, and Mom and Ted planned on staying awhile and meeting everyone. They didn't show up empty handed. Mom brought two large cakes, one chocolate and one white that she'd bought at a bakery shop. They were both delicious. Ted brought a large box filled with cold bottles of Eastside beer. They filled the ice bucket full, and the men around chopped up more ice and covered the already cold beer.

I introduced my family by saying, "They're here! Here they are! This is my mother, Julian; my daddy Ted; and my brother, Teddy Glen."

They didn't have any trouble getting acquainted. Mom and Ted didn't have any trouble filling their plates to the brim. They acted as though they were starved. There were extra plates around for anyone who forgot their plate or didn't know to bring his or her own.

The first thing our neighbors did was congratulate Mom and Ted on their entranceway. They had all been watching and wondering what on earth we were going to do.

They talked about it, shook their heads, made this comment and that. They laughed and seemed to know all about the driveway we were not allowed to use. Those people were not at the picnic.

Everyone loved my mother. She was the center of attention with funny stories about the cat show and stories about the cat owners. She just kept the group laughing.

Ted was on his fourth beer when he did a tumbling act for kids. He was very good, and he tried to show us how to do handstands. It was fun, and the "kids" loved it. However, I saw that plastic smile creeping up on Ted's face and I got melancholy and worried.

We were in and out of the water all day. Played games and my classroom acquaintances became my in-group. We bonded like a special family set apart from the world.

The kids in my hills knew all the secrets that leaked out of those coops. We shared them with each other-not gossip, just being in the know. It was the badge of belonging. We discussed situations and things that happened in the different families or what they found in one of the cesspools.

Our interpretations of sordid leaks were simplified to make sense according to our innocence. Our ignorance to understand what we heard was our own deep secret that we did not share as we pretended to understand by being shocked, delighted, or sorrowful.

Anyway, the stories we heard were just a matter of fact and another wonderment to envision and to steal our innocence away.

Our interpretation of one sordid story was that Lillian's mother went to the bathroom and a real live baby popped out of her and by accident she flushed the toilet; poor Lillian; she must be so sad.

The perfect day was coming to an end and cleanup began. People refilled their empty boxes with their dishes and belongings that they had brought.

The men broke apart the tables that had been doors and carried them to their truck. They emptied the tub of soft drinks and carried it to the truck. They turned the two fire rings into one big bomb fire.

No one took their chair just yet or removed the tub of beer. The kids all sat around the fire, and the babies were in their mama's lap or in a box made into a bed. People played the banjos and the fiddles and some danced, clapped and sang.

The folk songs ended with sadness about the severe dust storms that forced families to abandon their farms or employment not only in Arkansas but Oklahoma, Texas, and the Plains states.

If you listened you could almost feel the world's thorny switch whipping them after they enjoyed a good climate and good rainfall in the 1920's.

The next decade that came along was the driest. The drought was so severe that the topsoil became powdery, and the winds picked it up and blew it away. Some might say, "Well, they brought it on them selves with greedy farming practices." That might be partially true. It doesn't matter. They paid the consequences because of this fallen world, and they lost everything.

Close to four million people moved out of the Plains states. How many moved to California is unknown. I met a few people from Arkansas and even a few from Oklahoma in the hills just eight miles East of the Metropolitan city of Los Angeles.

Ted seemed to sober up, maybe because of all the food and activity. Mom was happy and I was the happiest of all. Teddy Glenn, Mama, and I went right to bed. Teddy Glen got to sleep with me. Ted stayed up to finish some beer that he brought back with him, and he played the piano into the night. I don't know how long he stayed up.

CHAPTER TWENTY

The tongue is small but it seems to control all. It leads our prayers, speaks of our cares and snares. Our tongue is as gentle as a lamb and complements all at hand. Regularly our tongue is out of control and divides the whole from any good goal. It starts a fire with a single spark that goes deep in the listener's heart. The tongue waggles its poison venom to destroy its victim. Only God can control the believers tongue.

My mother's tongue could entertain strangers and friends with stories of others and experiences of her own forever. She never told a sordid story accept to her sisters or husband. Her stories were funny, serious or sad and directed to the crowd for all to hear. She did not need to whisper in anybody's ear for friendship.

People loved her and followed her lead. She always said, "I can't keep a secret, so don't tell me any." That didn't matter. Someone was always whispering in her ear. They wanted to be her special friend. Mom never made a special friend. She always had a crowd of friends. Her special friends were her sisters and brothers.

Ted and Mom were talkative and pleased on the way home from the picnic. They mentioned that they had seen Dale, so they knew I was telling the truth about the boy with a peg leg running from the shed. They never said anything negative; it was my best day ever.

The next day I was told that I could never go into Lillian's house. Somebody blabbed the sordid story about her mother.

I innocently said that it was all just an accident and that she was real nice. Mom said, "I do not want you in her house, and that's final."

Julian started talking to Ted about it like I wasn't there. She used vocabulary that I did not know such as "miscarriages, and affairs." She made it sound awful and said that Mrs. Anderson ran around in the house naked with the shades up and no curtains.

I thought a lot about that, and every time I passed the house or walked home with Lil, I always looked in the windows expecting to see her naked. I never did.

December vacation was in sight and I was I looking forward to visiting my real daddy and my little sister.

November, December, January and February were considered the rainy season and it was here. Because we lived a little farther from the ocean and during the winter months I was in school, we didn't go to the ocean as often, but we still spent as much time as we could there.

That was Ted's favorite place and if Mom and Ted had a free Sunday, and it wasn't raining, we would leave just before noon drive thirty miles to the ocean and stay until the beaches closed at 10:00 pm.

Sometimes Ted fished off the pier. Sometimes I got to bring a friend, and we were free to run around all we wanted. The ocean was our family playground winter and summer.

There was no alcohol allowed on the beaches in California. We brought a day's worth of food to eat, and Ted always had his beer concealed in brown bags.

Every drop was drunk by 10:00 p.m. and he was as drunk as a skunk when we left. He drove home at a slow pace but always safe and sound.

I loved the evenings at the beach. The sunsets were incredible. We roasted weenies and marshmallows. Usually there was a church group or a big family close by sitting around their fire pits singing. We would listen and sing too, not with their group, but we would sing their songs with them, and it felt warm and friendly.

The rains did come in the winter, and many coops had leaky roofs. The men would get together and pour black tar on them. When that tar got hard, we "kids" would chew it like gum. Oh, how awful is that?

Ours never leaked because we had a new roof of hot tar and white gravel put on after the bathroom was completed.

Ted helped some other families whose roof was leaking, which was really against his temperament. He was not one to help people do yard work, paint, or work on a project, and would never loan out his van to help others. Ted was a Phlegmatic; unemotional, and just liked to watch what went on.

He was not one to encourage help for himself either. He liked to do everything himself with a cold beer at his side. He gladly accepted help with the bathroom, but he would have never asked for it. Uncle Allen and Ted's uncle Ray just came and did it. I think Julian made that happen.

Julian was the helper for anyone and for anything. These people were her new friends, and by "God" Ted was going to help and he did.

Mr. Theodore Tucker didn't have a clue, but he was going to be begging for help and advice from anyone before our rainy season was over.

Oh help, what are we supposed to do? The rains came down, and the cesspool crap came up, overflowed, and filled the yard. During this storm, we did not enjoy the smell of the sweet rain but instead we smelled the foul noxious odor emanating from over flowing cesspools everywhere. It was a mess. The more it rained, the worse it got, and when the rain stopped, it took a long time for the red mud to absorb the foul water.

The cesspool is thought to be a buried tank with an open bottom to hold waste. Most of the cesspools in our hills did not have a tank.

We just dug into the red clay that formed our hills with a shovel and a pick. We dug a round hole in the ground about twelve feet deep and about four feet wide with a sealed safety top that constantly over flowed.

Abandon holes on property was common as a new one was being dug with hopes that it would be more absorbent. Usually boards covered the top of the abandoned hole, and we kids were warned about them. Even so, every year someone fell in or our pet fell into a half empty dirty, smelly hole. Because they were not fenced and not on a leach they would sometimes stray from home and end up in an abandon hole.

Ted was advised to dig another hole right by the one he had and install a sewer pipe twenty inches from the top. When the first hole filled up, it would run over to the second hole. The solid waste would stay in the bottom of the first hole. The liquid would come to the top of the first hole and flow to the second hole. Now the cesspools would not over flow if the tops were sealed so the rain could not fill them. And that was the end of our trouble.

Ted started digging. It was quite an operation. First he found a used winch that was used to draw water out of a well. He put a new rope on it, and it was like new. It wasn't long before the hole was deep enough that Ted had to lower a bucket down to my mother. She was down inside the hole picking and digging it deeper. Mom would fill a large bucket with the dirt. Ted would draw it up with the winch and dump it, lower it back down to her and he would spread the dirt with a rake. My job was to take care of Teddy Glenn.

When Mom went in to fix dinner, she took Teddy Glenn with her. Ted threw a couple of buckets in the hole. I would climb down the ladder, pick at the dirt, and fill the buckets.

I could not lift them to the hook, so I just got them ready to be pulled up while Ted set up a light so they could work after dark.

One particular evening while I was filling the buckets, Ted climbed into the hole, grabbed me, pulled up my dress, and jacked him self off on me. I screamed at him and pushed him away. He didn't say anything. He just climbed the ladder as though nothing had happened, and Mom called us for dinner.

I didn't know what to do, or how to act. Ted acted normal, hungry, and pleasant. I was starved earlier, but now I didn't feel hungry at all. I felt nauseated. I felt hurt. I don't know if the feeling I had was hate. I didn't know hate yet but I cried inside of my body.

Very few people had phones in the 1940's. There were a few types of professions that had them, and of course the railroad employees, rooming houses, and whatever was deemed necessary did have them. Unless it was arranged ahead of time, there was no way to be notified that you were about to have company. Friends and family was very abusive to each other with unannounced visits.

Sometimes these visits were great because you got out of planed chores, and instead you had cousins or friends to play with. Sometimes they were disappointing because you were just about to leave for something special that had been planned.

One thing for sure was that the kids better never say they were just leaving or treat any guest with less then a sincere smile that said, "Oh, we are so happy to see you."

The dinner hour was no exception, at least for family on the weekends. Maybe that is why it was so common to have stew, oxtail soup, or some kind of beef soup, potato soup, chili beans, or spaghetti, and most always a pot of beans with a ham hock cooking on the stove. Food was never wasted, and we always seem to have enough. Ted and Julian enjoyed company, and it usually gave Ted an excuse to go to the liquor store and restock his beer. After dinner Pinochle was usually in order.

My 3:00 p.m. curfew was not enforced when my cousins were there. We just had to be home before dark. We usually went to the rolling hills across from our coop and played war.

When the adults started their Pinochle game, we stayed out of their way with hopes of not being remembered so as not having to go to bed.

It was Saturday afternoon when Aunt Caroline drove up with Ralph and the kids, all but Howe. Howe didn't go anywhere with them anymore. He was older now, and it's all he thought about was leaving home and joining the Navy. Caroline didn't make him do much that he didn't want to do. She just wanted to keep him from running off.

Caroline hollered down for my Mom and Ted to come up and help her get Ralph down the stairs. He was on crutches. He had a shocking dark bruise that covered his forehead down to the tip of his nose, and had two black eyes. He was dressed in a stripped dark suit with one pant leg cut off at the middle of his thigh. He was wearing a cast on his foot up past his ankle, which was broken. He wore a tie and had on a felt hat. He looked miserable.

The kids carried down a large box that contained a ham and four loafs of home made bread. Mom did have a pan of red beans cooking on the stove, and it all smelled so good. I was starved, but it would be awhile before we ate.

Aunt Caroline said that last Tuesday, the police found Ralph unconscious by a path leading down to the Los Angeles River.

There didn't seem to be any foul play. His wallet was in tack and undisturbed, and he smelled of alcohol. They thought he twisted his foot in a small crevasse, which threw him hard to the ground.

Ralph had a different story. He said that he was going down by the River to walk along the path, and Howe came up behind him and buckled both legs, causing him to fall.

Ralph didn't actually see him, but he could smell him and felt his presence.

Howe acted offended and outraged that Ralph dare to accuse him. He said he had no right to try and finger him. He already lived in his Dad's house; how much more did he want?

Caroline said that Howe hated Ralph and had threatened to kill him. She wanted to know if we would take him until he recovered. "After all, Ted, he is your father, and I can't work and take care of him.

I have always opened my home to you, Ted, and now it's my turn. Ralph has got to go. I love him, but I won't have my children accused of such a heinous crime. I am going to divorce him.

CHAPTER TWENTYONE

The world's thorny switch makes families twitch and shudder and sometimes wonder if they should sunder. It makes me wonder where I would be if it weren't for my family that took care of me. They were not perfect people. You see, they lived in a fallen world like you and like me.

"Oh shit Caroline, hell no we won't take him." "Where is your mind? Where is he going to sleep? Where do we hang his twenty suits, and white shirts, and stack his twenty pair of shoes? Oh for crying out loud, show us where we should store his boxes of handkerchief, under ware, and ties. Damn, I can't believe this. Yes, he is my father, but he is your husband, so what happened to: for better, or, for *worse***,** for richer, for poorer, in *sickness and in health,* to love and to cherish, till death do us part?"

Ted continued, "Hell, he can't even get up the stairs by himself. It will probably be three to four months before that cast comes off. Maybe the County will help him until then. After that, he can take care of himself just like he has always done."

Ralph was weeping on the couch. "Caroline doesn't love me anymore. My own son doesn't love me, and my stepsons wish I were dead. I have no one now. What have I ever done to deserve this?"

Caroline said, "Well I'll be damned. After all I have done for Julian and Peggy. She and Peggy would have been in the street if it weren't for Bernie and me."

Ted said, "No Caroline, you would have stayed home and taken care of your family. There is no one else in this world that would have taken care of your four kids and done the housework, the washing, and ironing for food and a bed. Oh no, Caroline, Julian did you a favor. Julian could have gone to work in one day. The papers were full of Ad's, and she would have received room and board and a paycheck."

Marylou and I were sitting on the floor, coloring and listening to every word. The boys were told to go outside and play, they were at the door listening, complaining that they were hungry and wanted to come in.

Caroline was shocked at what Ted said and especially the tone he used. It was a couple of seconds before she replied, "Don't you speak to me that way, Ted. I was damn good to Julian; I never took advantage of her. I shared everything, and when we went someplace, we always took her with us and paid their way. She is my sister and I love her, and Peggy, you seemed to have been happy there."

"I was happy, Caroline, and I paid my way," said Ted. "I know that when Julian left your home, you had to let Marylou live with Virginia and Paul. I know that the lady you've hired does lighthouse work only, and half way watches Henry and Herb.

She does not wash clothes, make beds, or iron. She eats all she wants and receives a paycheck. You should be complementing Julia and telling her how much you miss her instead of telling her you did her a favor."

Caroline did not reply. Ted continued, "It will be another year before we build another bedroom, and we sure as hell will not be building it for my dad".

Julian said, "Enough of this nonsense. I appreciate all that you did for me; sis, and I know that you appreciated my hard work. Caroline, we have one bedroom that Ted and I sleep in with Teddy Glen in his crib next to the wall, and Peggy sleeps in the living room. You have two empty rooms not used at all. I suggest you make one of those rooms into a den for Ralph.

Except for getting his lunch out of the icebox and using the bathroom, he should promise to stay in his den until you get home from work. Of course, if the "Kid's are not there, he can roam around, but never in their bedroom."

Ralph still weeping. "Oh, Caroline, I will do anything for you, I love you. I can't live without you. I promise that I will not leave my room until you get home, not until I get rid of this cast, except to use the bathroom and to get something out of the icebox, I won't even sit at the kitchen table until you get home".

Julian continued, "He has to keep his promise that he will not criticize the kids, accuse Howe, or even talk to them. If he does, kick him out. The County might help him. After his cast comes off you can decide what to do."

This seemed to cool things down for Caroline and her attitude changed. She said, "I am sorry, I know you can't take him. Good grief, where would he sleep? I should not have brought my problems for you to solve anyway. I love Ralph. We enjoy each other, and he shows me a lot of affection and love. He does a lot of things around the house for us. He expects the boy's to keep the yard up, and trouble starts there a lot of times."

"Well, if he keeps his promise, it will be up to you, sis, to make the boys do their chores and things just might turn around."

Let's eat, and maybe after dinner we could prop Ralph up for a Pinochle game or two."

Ralph blubbered a pleasant grunt, nodding his head, "Yes, yes," He said he was hurting a little bit and took a swig of Jack Daniel."

There was no depression or gloominess at the table. No one could have guessed they just finished a pretty good yelling match.

We were all hungry, and the red beans and ham, canned spinach, and homemade bread were exceptionally good. Well maybe not the canned spinach.

There was no desert, so Ted gave us a nickel to buy an ice cream bar at Tinker's. On the way, Marylou said, "Boy they sure said some bad words. Do you think they will go to hell for saying them?"

Herb said, "Hell no. I know more bad words than what they said, and Howe knows more than me."

Henry said, "Yeah, "me too, and God hasn't sent us to hell. Do you want to hear some?"

I said, "My Mother says it hurts God's ears to say bad words, so when I get mad I just say, "Oh Corn,' or that's corny or just 'corn."

CHAPTER TWENTYTWO

I love the Trinity the Godhead of all eternity. He gives me His Joy, and He holds my hand tight with every burden, inversion, and fright. Thank you, Lord for my emotions and sensations. They have saved my life on many occasions. He never leaves me when I am not right but instead leads me to His Light. What a joy, what a sight to be in His light.

*I*n 1942, the war that was raging was hell for those soldier boys. Almost 150,000 Allied soldiers became deserters before the war was over. They had a story too because they were part of the war.

No one wants to hear their story they have been judged cowards. Most of them were combat troops who were ten percent of its total army. They were in the front lines, seldom being rotated by other units for rest.

They suffered grief at the continuous replacement of their dead, and they lived with the trauma of constant terror and fear of landmines and endless battle.

They fought, and some won decorations for courage and even the silver and bronze star before they deserted, but broke down psychologically before the end. Traumatized men were sent back to the front lines.

Judge not, I believe that each person has their limits no matter how strong they are mentally and physically. Can we even know our own limit? What would I do if I threw a grenade in a building and out comes a child whose arms I just blew off?

I am persuaded that few deserters were cowards. I believe most broke down or was pushed beyond their limits. They had to face the enemy without let-up for many months.

Disgrace, or death I wonder which I would choose? I would pray that it would be death for my country, but how could I know? Dare I to judge?

I feel the same about police officers. There are some bad apples, but most of them put their lives on the line to protect us everyday.

Two of my uncles enlisted in the Army before the war broke out. Both uncles became deserters. One got caught, and the other one was never caught.

Mom's younger brother but not the youngest deserted in 1943. And was not caught until 1954. I don't know his story. No one talked about it. Grandma took her stars out of the window.

Most families don't talk about a disgraceful thing that their child or a sibling did unless they have a better story to prove it wasn't their fault, and then they never shut up about it. There were no cover-up stories for deserters. They were considered a disgrace.

I didn't know Uncle John was a deserter until he went to prison. Uncle John, as far as I knew, was a truck driver. I was too young to wonder why he was no longer in the service before the war was over; I never thought about it.

John fell madly in love with Ted's sister Irene. They became a couple, and he found a two-bedroom house for them to include the boy's: Bobby, Larry and Jimmy. Their father was happy to get rid of them, and John planned on raising them as his own with his new baby girl.

Aunt Irene had a beautiful baby girl she named Jane. The DNA in that baby girl would surly make a forensic team think that she and her cousin Teddy Glenn were brother and sister.

Ted and Irene were biological brother and sister, and John and Julian were biological brother and sister. Ted said they were more closely related than Teddy Glenn and me. I cried because he was my brother, but now he had another who was closer. That was probably my first feeling of jealousy.

Irene's boys really liked John. He was good to them, and they had a good relationship. Everyone liked John he was like an identical twin to my Mother. They looked alike, and he had the same personality as she did. He was tall and handsome, liked western music, and had an unusual vibrato tenor voice and loved to sing.

He was a ladies man, and if that was the reason, I don't know, but John and Irene didn't stay together very long, and the boys were shifted back to their father for a while.

It was probably two years after John remarried. and changed his trucking Co employment when the military caught up with him. He had a baby boy and another on the way.

He spent two years in prison. His wife waited for him. She was a practical nurse. She put in extra hours and study, and obtained her LVN while her husband served his time.

Their two boys were only a year older than my two boys. They bought a home in Norwalk, California, and we bought a home in LA Mirada, California, maybe ten miles a part, but we never became close. John was twelve years older than his wife, Jo Ann, and eighteen years older than me. We did have our boys in common but nothing else.

Every time I looked at him, I remembered the two times he got me a lone when I was very young and told me that I made up that story about Ted, and I should be a shamed of my self.

John had a motorcycle, and when his boys were in their early teens he taught them to ride it. One day he let the oldest boy ride the motorcycle on their street by himself. He lost control, ran it into a tree just four houses down from theirs, and was killed instantly.

About four months latter, John had a major heart attack and was left with an inoperable aneurism.

In a shot few months, his youngest boy decided to take the motorcycle for a ride without his father or mother knowing. He got off their street on to Norwalk Boulevard, ran into a car, and was killed instantly. It was horrible. It was unbelievable. That motorcycle had not been touched since their oldest boy was killed on it.

In the same year John's aneurism burst, and he died. Jo Ann lost both of her young sons and her husband in that one horrible year.

The world's thorny switch beat her until she cried so long that her tears became dry. She left her job, sold their home and moved out of state to be by her sister. She wrote my mother a couple of letters, and then we never heard from her again. I think about her often. She would be ninety-eight, so she may have passed by now,

Jo Ann was very nice to me, and I liked her very much. She was a good wife and a good mother. She was always sweet but not a phony. Her family was fortunate to have her.

Mom's baby brother, Fred, was on the front lines a long time. He was injured got a leave after a short hospital stay. He got drunk, overstayed his leave, and was picked up for being out of uniform and AWOL. He was brought back, punished, and put back on the front of the lines.

Fred was blown out of a foxhole and injured quite severely. He also contacted malaria and was in the hospital for quite some time. He came home on leave. He was shell-shocked and stuttered, which he had never done before. He again went AWOL and after thirty days was considered deserted. He stayed a deserter and he changed his name Social Security number, and driver's license. He married, and he and his wife had a little girl, he drove truck and he never was caught.

I had six cousins whom I know about who served in war: four in the Navy, one in the Army, and one in the Marines. None of them deserted, but there is not one of them who were not affected. War is a terrible experience. I thank these men and women who have fought for our country, all of them. Because of them, we have the chance to prosper. And we did, and our family has succeeded.

CHAPTER TWENTYTHREE

The fruit of the vine fermented becomes wine for some to drink as they dine, pine and sometimes act like a swine. Fermentation converts sugar to acids and gases that smell rancid. But the context of Scripture is a picture of our Savior, who teaches us much better behavior and is so much greater.

I have been asked many times, "Why did Jesus turn water into wine if He didn't want us to drink it? Well, I don't know Hebrew, and I don't know Greek. I have researched the word *wine,* and I am persuaded that it has more than one meaning and that Jesus turned water into the pure fruit of the vine. However, you couldn't prove it by me; I have yet to master English.

I might ask a better question: "Why would Jesus want us to drink anything that would decrease our resistance to our proclivities?" We all have proclivities. There is no one that is without them, and through our years we learn what they are. They are not approved of by God or in any society or culture. In fact, some of our proclivities could send us to prison.

Our platitude or cliché today is: "we were born that way"

Well, for sure we are born with a sin nature. We are born that way, but according to the Bible, sin does not have dominion over us. We are not in bondage to it.

It is a proven fact that alcohol affects our judgment, behavior, passions, temper, and our morality. In context, the Scriptures teach us to be like Jesus. We could never be like Jesus under the influence of alcohol. For Jesus to turn water into fermented wine would be in contradiction to His character and out of context to Scripture.

Mr. Theodor Tucker was good to me at first and I don't believe he intended to marry my mother with the purpose to destroy my relationship with her or hurting me.

I am not an expert on pedophilia. I am aware that the definition of pedophilia is someone who sexually abuses children. It may well have been one of Ted's proclivities that alcohol facilitated for him to act upon.

I think his sexual abuse was more resentment for me, than a sex desire. I think it thrilled him that he could get away with it. I don't think it was about power in his case. I think Ted thought, *why should I be burdened with James Kid?* There is usually more than just one reason a person gives away to their proclivities.

Ted was cruel to me in other ways too. I was the one who had to touch the concession machines to see if there was a short in them before the set up. He would be connecting the power, and Mom would be setting up the stock. Some one had to do it. But I was only nine and had gotten shocked more than once, so I responded with fear, jerking my hand back several times before touching the machine. This seemed to thrill Ted and he would laugh and say, "You act like a baby", or he would be angry because it took too long to touch the machine.

When I got the mumps, Ted brought me a dill pickle and told me to suck on it and it would make me feel better. It really hurt, and he laughed and laughed. He did things like that.

He never whipped me or hit me. He did slap me a couple of times but he wasn't one to hit. My friends were always welcome, and if possible, he and Mom were willing to take us here or there. The icebox was always open to us, and my friends thought my parents were really nice. Today they would say were "awesome" or" cool."

I think the burden for me was a broken relationship with my mother. We were never close after I told her what Ted had done to me. Mom believed me but wanted to believe Ted as he suggested many times that it was James, my father that sexually abused me. That was not true. Mom just wanted it all to go away, she wanted to pretend that it never happened.

I was to call Ted, Daddy, out of respect. Mom continued to leave me alone with him. My mother would send me off to the store with Ted or work a concession event alone with him. She left me without protection or security.

Another burden for me was the un-trustfulness, and coldness from my Aunts whom I loved so much and wanted them to love me. They believed Ted, and thought I was a liar or that my father James was the one who did it.

It seemed to me that calling him Daddy was the same thing as saying, "It didn't really happen." I resented that because it did happen and my real daddy didn't do that. It was like a pretend game to acknowledge and respect his position in my life and I acquiesced to the command.

I told on him several times, but he always denied it and said, "Take her to the doctor and see. I never touched her. And if she has been touched, it was from her father, not by me."

Mom would look so hurt and confused and she would relate everything to her brothers and sisters, and they would reassure her that if Ted did anything to me, he wouldn't tell her to take me to the doctor.

I didn't know anything about intercourse so I didn't understand what they meant. If I had, I am sure I could have better explained what Ted was doing to me. I just knew that what he was doing was bad and always made me feel nauseated.

I loved my mother, and I worried that she thought I was a liar. I thought that if I had not been born, she would not be going through this. I was causing her so much pain. I wished I had never told, and yet I told her again and again.

Family was important to me. I loved my brother, Teddy Glenn, and all my aunt's uncles and cousins. I wanted my boy's to have grandparents and to know our family. I wanted my mother to have grandchildren and to appreciate them. They would be the best grandchildren in the world.

Because I played the game, it kept our family together and Ted didn't come after me as much when I got older and not at all after I was married, so I didn't have to deal with that part anymore. I played the game until he died.

Ted was good to me in many ways, and I don't think he would have violated me if I had been his own daughter. He kept a roof over my head; he bought my clothes and shoes, school supplies, vacations; and paid for my medical care or anything that I needed. He brought music and art in the house and he taught me many things.

I forgive him and believe that he found rest in Jesus and is in heaven. It's hard for any of us to get through this fallen world without giving way to a proclivity or two.

We are quick to label proclivities such as, "I would never do that." Well, if you don't have that particular proclivity, you wouldn't. Perhaps your proclivity is murder or maybe you are secretly a kleptomaniac, a troublemaker, a gossip, an alcoholic, a drug addict, prideful, narcissist, sex perversion, there is no end to sin. And according to the Bible, one sin is no worse than the other in that all sins goes against God. . When sin hurts a child we all cringe, and think that has to be a worse sin then all the others. I thank God that is not my proclivity and thank Him for paying the penalty for all my sins and weaknesses.

We are just like our parents Adam and Eve. Eve said that the snake made me do it. Adam said that Eve talked me into it. And we say, "It's my dad's fault or it's my mom's fault." If they would have done this or not done that we would be better. It's their fault. And our parents say it was their parent's fault. And their parents say it was their parent's fault. Too bad for Adam and Eve when we all get to heaven-if they made it, that is. There is no record that they ever repented.

Everyone in the whole world has a burden or will before they die. My special friend, Dale, had a terrible burden that he lived with everyday until the end.

CHAPTER TWENTYFOUR

Don't worry we survived mercury. We only made a fuss when the asbestos celling made a little dust. We survived suns fiery severity without the help of sunscreens security. Chewing led pencils and eating the yellow paint seemed to digest with all the rest.

We chewed black road tar, Bee's wax, and Fleers bubble gum, and only our teachers grumbled and caused us trouble. Breathing exhaust fumes with leaded gas gave us a blast of nausea that would last until we thought we passed.

"We shouldn't have lasted," blasted the news. So don't be telling our "kid's your eight six and eighty two. Don't tell them your past. They don't have a clue that potatoes fried in bacon grease are what to do for the taste and not one potato will be a waste.

We followed the ice truck that comes every day. He'll soon drop some ice our way. We'll stomp it, chomp it, and munch it down after it turns brown from the dirt on the ground.

Red beans fried in lard we no longer should eat it's another warning we'll die in the morning. White flower is out; white bread is out; white potatoes are a sin even if they are sliced thin.

Dale was having trouble learning to read. Mrs. Harnicor, our fourth grade teacher, always called him to read out loud in front of the class. The class would snicker and put their hand over their mouth.

Dale said, "no." a couple of times, and Mrs. Harnicor sent a letter home to his parents. He never refused again, and I knew why. He would get whipped in the chicken coop with a chicken.

He probably wouldn't have cared if it had only got switched with a peach or an apricot switch, but a chicken was unbearable, and he was left with terrible cuts and burses.

"Dale," I called, "Wait a minute, I want to tell you something. I have to go straight home after school, so I can't walk the long way home with you today. If you will walk me by my house I will tell you something."

"What is it? I can't walk a girl home, Peggy. Tell me now." "No, it will take to long. And anyway, you don't have to act like you're walking with me. Please, Dale."

Oh, all right. But it'd better be good. Let's go. Okay, tell me."

"I am going to tell you how to read, and no body will ever laugh at you again, especially Dotty the Dot, she thinks she is so smart. It's a secret, Dale, and as soon as you know the secret, you will be able to read as well as anyone in the class, and Mrs. Harnicor will drop dead of a heart attack".

"Okay, tell me the secret." "It will take more than one day, maybe more than five days".

"I am not going to walk any girl home for five days."

"Even if you will be able to read as good as Dot or me? Mom might let me walk the long way home a couple of days. Come on, Dale, you just have too."

"Start telling me, and then I will decide."

"Okay, here goes. Each letter makes one sound, and a few make two or three sounds at the most. If you know the sound, the letters make, you can read. Like your name starts with *D*, and the *D* says, 'duh'. My name starts with a *P*, and the *P* says, 'puh'".

'"PUGGY?" "

"No, you don't know the sound of the *E* yet. Now, listen, this really works. Just try, it will be fun".

"Yeah, fun for you, it sounds like hogwash to me."

"No, it will be fun watching Mrs. Harnicor drop dead with a heart attack. There is only one other thing you have to say, and that is *A, E, I, O, U and sometimes Y.* Those are vowels."

Mom let me walk Dale home the next day, and he was anxious to tell me he remembered what the *D* say's and what the *P* says, and he said, *"A, E, I, O, U"* real fast and ran ahead.

I caught him. He wanted to know how you could get *Dale* out of duh so we worked on the letter *A* and *E* next. We learned that when two vowels walk together, the first one does the talking and the second one does the walking. Some words we just have to learn because they don't follow any rules. Names don't have to follow rules.

Dale wanted to know everything about letters. It was like a game to him. He was like a blind person getting their sight. He was so quick to understand how to use the sounds that I can't help but wonder how he got to fourth grade without learning to read.

When I got home my Mother said that they got a letter from Mrs. Harnicor saying that I didn't know my multiplication tables, and if I didn't learn them this year I would not be able to divide or learn fractions next year.

I thought I was going to get switched, but instead Mom said "you will know them *tomorrow*. "That was the worse night of my life, and it was still going on at 2:30 A.M.

I formed a block on at least three of them and when asked what was 6 x7, 7 x 8, 9 x 8, I would start shaking. I was afraid to give the answer because if it were wrong *again* they both would go into a hissy fit and kill me.

At 2:30 a.m., I said my timetables correctly and got to go to bed. I knew them better than anyone in the world and could say them faster then anyone. We even had races at school. Two kids would stand together, the teacher would ask the timetable, and the one who answered first won. I always won forever after.

I asked Dale if he knew his multiplication tables and he said, "pretty good. They're kind of easy. Twos through fives, you can just add them up. Nines, the answer starts with one less than it's times. I like arithmetic I got a B on my report card."

"Wow, that's great. I got a C-minus. And Mom said I was not paying attention, that I was daydreaming in class, and she made me get a switch from the peach tree. She switched me for getting a minus. I hate report card day."

Dale said, "Well, now that you know your time tables, Mrs. Harnicor will have to give you an A and have a heart attack." "Yeah," I said.

Dale did learn his sounds and how to use them. I told him that the *A* in his name had three sounds because the *A* thought it was special. And it would go around saying it's own name whenever it could. "*A* does that in your name, Dale. It likes to hear its own name." Dale smiled big,

He loved playing with the sounds and the vowels. He looked puzzled when I asked him what *O* and *W* said together, so I pinched him and he responded, "Ow."

I said, "Right."

Now Mrs. Harnicor smiled when Dale read out loud because she thought she was the one teaching him to read. How could she think she was teaching him anything by making him make a fool of himself in front of the class?

When Dale was through reading, he always looked at me, and that smile just spread across his face. The kids no longer snickered at him. Our fourth grade problems were solved, and it gave us more time to be wild and play.

I wanted to be part of Dorothy the Dot's clique. I wanted to be recognized as one of them too. Knowing my Multiplication tables so well opened the door a little bit. Dot was usually one of the leaders to pick sides. She picked the smartest ones to be on her side, when choosing up sides, for a game in arithmetic, spelling or what ever.

"Dorothy, I said, "Do you want to come over to my house after school? We could go to my pond and play with pollywogs."

"I can't, I have chores after school."

"I do too, maybe after your chores".

"That's not your pond, Peggy. It belongs to everyone. We have a picnic sometimes after Mass at the pond.

"What is Mass?" I asked?

"That's what we do in our church. We're Catholic. What church do you go to?" she asked.

"The Foursquare church on Pain Ave."

Dot said," Oh my gosh, that's the Holy Roller's church."

I said," What do you mean?"

"They roll on the floor," she answered.

"No they don't, I never saw anyone roll on the floor.

"My Mother said that they dance and roll on the floor.

Anyway, I could never come to your house. My mother says only Arkies and Okies live in those hills, and they stay barefoot and have to go to the bathroom in an outhouse. All their houses are dumps, not much better than chicken coops.

My Mother says that there is a crazy man who lives up there and lives in the chicken coop with the chickens and howls at night.

She said that they found two little babies floating in a big hole full of smelly dirty water, and I was never to go in those hills."

"But none of that is true Dorothy. We have a real nice bathroom, we don't use an outhouse, and the people in our church don't roll on the floor. Sometimes I go to church with Lillian, the church that is by "Tinkers". Lillian sings solo sometimes."

"I don't know "Tinkers or the church because we're Catholic. We don't go to other kinds of churches".

"I like to skate. Do you want to go skating with me some time Dottie?

Yes, but I have to ask my Mother first." Maybe you can come over to my house after school tomorrow. I'll ask my mother if you can."

"Okay, I'll ask if I can come. I will bring my skates if she says yes.

I didn't get to go because we had to work at a school carnival that evening. It was only a three-hour job, and we should have been home by 9:00 p.m., but we didn't get home until much latter.

Ted never drank at the school carnivals, so he usually did most everything but the clean up. There was not much for me to do but watch Teddy Glenn, and he usually went to sleep in a bed Mom made for him in the van. There was seldom money to find on the ground because the "Kids all used tickets for what they wanted. At the end of the evening, we just turned the tickets in for our money.

On the way home, we stopped to get bread, milk, and eggs at Safeway, but before Ted and Mom got out of the car, a man with a mask stuck a gun in Ted's window and said, "Put your hands on the stirring wheel." He opened the door reached in and took Mom's purse. He seemed to know we carried a moneybag, and where it was. He never asked for Ted's wallet he just took Mom's purse, and the moneybag, and disappeared.

We waited there for the police, and they said that it sounded as though we had been followed. Ted and Mom were really distressed and worried for some time because whoever it was seemed to be familiar with our van and who was inside.

They suspected someone at the Carnival had been watching us, and when we left they followed.

The thing Ted was concerned about was that the robber had a gun and evidently intended to follow us home. There is no way he could have known we were going to stop at the store. The thought of him following us home with a gun was scary, and we became much more cautious of our surroundings at the different events forever after.

CHAPTER TWENTYFIVE

Trees and bumblebees awaken and beckon for spring. Easter is near, and I can hear the honeybees singing clear. Shorter nights with a longer day expose children at play, and the wild flowers' appearance are soon on their way with their endurance to try and give us assurance that all is okay for another day. An unusual summer was approaching our way as well as the world's thorny switch to be on display.

I didn't get to visit my Father at Easter because he had been drafted in the army, or he may have enlisted. He was older than Ted and Ted had not been drafted yet. I was so proud and wished I could put a star somewhere so everyone would know.

It was just before Easter break. It was time for my teacher to have teacher parent conference. I overheard Mom telling Ted that Mrs. Harnicor said that she didn't understand me, that I would disobey rules like chewing gum, talking during class, or moving during the silent bell. Then I would proceed to tell her about it with an attitude of, "What are you going to do about it?"

I heard a lot of things Ted and Mom talked about if I sat on the floor pretending to be coloring. Marylou taught me how to do that.

Ted said, "For Christ Sake, I told you that you shouldn't be telling her to tell you when she did some damn thing wrong before Jesus did. That is why she is telling on herself.

She thinks Jesus is going to tell the teacher." He then laughed and laughed. "She is to old to be believing that anyway, Julian. That is the most ridiculous thing I have ever heard." He laughed some more. "I don't want you to be telling Teddy Glenn such a preposterous notion."

I was puzzled, and I thought about what he said for a while. But I soon tucked it away to think about for another time. I would surly know better by the end of fifth grade. At least I hoped I would know what ever it was that I was too old not to know.

The last day of school in June meant our report cards would be passed out for the end of that year. I knew I would get an A in arithmetic and an A in reading.

I was all smiles, and very talkative, and anxious for the half-day to end. But my smile turned to worry and my eyes to tears. I got a B in reading and a C+ plus in arithmetic– not one A on my report-card and worse was a note on the bottom of it that read, "Needs improvement and talks to much in class". I hated report card day I always got elevator stomach.

That teacher is mean, I thought. I know my timetables better than she does, and Dottie and I are the best readers in the class. Dottie the Dot reads books all the time and is always telling Mrs. Harnicor. I only read what I have to because I like to skate and play, and there just isn't enough time for both.

Dale was so happy when he saw his card. It made me forget about my fear long enough to be excited with him. He got a B in arithmetic and an A in reading with a note on the bottom that read "Greatly Improved." I was happy for him and thought his daddy would be so proud and be sorry that he whipped him with chickens.

The last day of school was only a half-day, so Mom said I could go with my girlfriends after school. We had the day planned, but now I didn't want to go. I wanted to go home and get my switching over with.

I brought my report card home right away. Mom and Ted were both sitting at the kitchen table drinking coffee and looking very serious. They just glanced at me as I gingerly laid my report card on the table. Mom asked why I was home early. "I want to get my skates," I said.

Ted looked at my report card and said, "You brought your arithmetic up by a whole grade. That is good."

I guess I didn't take into consideration that I was still counting on my fingers to add and subtract. I smiled.

Mom said, "If you didn't talk in class, you would have a very good report card, young lady."

"Mom, I am not going to talk in class next year, I promise."

Julian said that she wouldn't mind having tamale from the tamale wagon down by Echo Park, and maybe we could take a walk around the lake and stop by and visit Grandma Tucker.

There were food wagons in the Metropolitan Los Angeles area, and every now and then Mom would get hungry for their tamales covered with chili beans. They were delicious.

We never got bored with the walk around Echo Park Lake. About half way around were motorboats for people to rent. We could never do that, but sometimes Ted would buy us peanuts or a candy bar at the boat launch, and we would watch the boats before continuing the rest of the route. Then we would go to Grandma Tuckers to visit her and Irene, who lived with her, and I would always hope in vain that Bobby, Larry and Jimmy would be there.

Mom was still switching me often, I know I deserved most of them for disobeying, and then I would tell on my self with probably the same attitude Mrs. Harnicor said I had. It seemed as though my Mother was constantly angry with me until the day she died.

I was not an easy child. I was forever pleading to see my father, or begging to go home if we were at some ones house and Ted started on his third beer. I knew there would be a fight between Mom and him about going home, and I would start in that I had a headache or I was sick at my stomach. Ted would seethe at me with a look that could kill.

For another example: One time when I was eight or nine, Ted had invited three of his boyhood friends and their wives over for a party. That meant getting drunk. Julian had decorated the coop and gotten a new dress. They bought snacks and everything else for parties in that day, to include large bottles of liquor. When the guess arrived they had brought liquor too.

I don't remember all the small details, but this I remember vividly. After their third round of drinks and Ted's face started transforming into his plastic smile, I slipped into the kitchen, poured a portion of the liquor from the open bottles down the drain, and filled them with water to the level they had been at.

Thinking back to that night it makes me a true believer that after a couple of drinks, the taste buds are numb, and no matter what you drink after that you wouldn't know the difference.

The party ended early, no one seemed too inebriated, just a little happy, even though they emptied their bottles, but I made several trips to the kitchen.

I always told on myself, and the next day as I was helping my mother clean up after the party, I told her what I did and maybe with an attitude, I don't know, I just had to tell her first. What would you do with a "Kid" like that?

The pond was where our social gatherings always took place. Everyone respected it and the area around it. Each person felt it was his or her special pond, and it was amazingly clean, always ready for the next event. We brought our trash in, and we took it out. We have had many picnics there since the first one I attended, and many stories have been added to my Arkie and Okie Family.

This year we got two new families, one from Kansas and one from Missouri: "Bart and Emma Hayes with four girls and twin boys from Kansas, Ted's Uncle Ray and Aunt Ida May Taylor with a grown daughter, Maryanne, from Missouri.

The Hayes girls were stair step in age, and one was my age.

Both families bought empty lots and started building. Both of them built two-story houses not dumps. Well, they were sort of dumps in that the families built them on their own, a little at a time, and no one was a carpenter. Both families camped out on their property all summer while they built. Both men held full time jobs, so it was a slow process.

Ted and Julian seldom got to go to the picnics because concession work is mostly on the weekends. They let me go by my self if they didn't need me to take care of Teddy Glenn, and sometimes I got to stay over night with one of my girlfriends whose family attended the picnic and invited me.

One summer morning when I woke up, I had a dark, depressed feeling fall over me. I even felt that I wanted to cry. Nothing was wrong that I knew about, but I couldn't shake it.

It was early, Mom and Ted were sleeping, and I brought Teddy Glenn into the kitchen, fed some Corn Flakes, and played with him until Mom got up. She started Ted's big breakfast, and I walked outside.

I heard Dale calling me down by the shed. There he was laying in the grass with his shirt half torn off and bloody.

He was in the chicken coop with his crazy drunken father last night. He had really gotten it; He had welts across his left ribs and a cut on the left side of his neck. I couldn't see right away where all the blood came from, but when I got close, I could see a deep cut on his side. Luckily most of the blood had coagulated, but the one on his side continued to ooze.

"You need to come into the house, Dale, Mom will help you."

"No Peggy, I don't want anyone to know that my father is a crazy ass. I am going to kill him you'll see".

No, don't talk like that. If you kill him, you will go to hell."

"Why do you say that Peggy? What hell?

"There is a heaven and a hell. If you're good, you go to heaven with Jesus, and if you're bad, you go hell with the devil" I answered.

"I never heard that. When we get mad, we say, "Go to hell.' That's all it means."

You have been here all night, haven't you? "I asked.

"Yes. I was going to get into the shed, but it's locked."

"I know. Ted has all his concession machines and stock in there. Oh Dale, you have to let Mom see you. She won't tell. You need to have all your cuts cleaned and have iodine and bandages put on them. Please Dale."

"No Peggy, I won't."

"Okay, Dale. I will get a bucket of warm water and soap and clean your cuts.

"No soap."

"Yes. We'll rinse the soap off with the hose.

 I will throw your shirt in the incinerator, and you can put a towel around you."

"Oh, Peggy, you are my best friend, but don't ever tell anyone. My best friend can't be a girl."

"I won't, Dale. You are my best friend too, and I don't want you to go to hell."

"I am so sleepy, and I feel sick," he said.

"After I clean you up, I think you can go to sleep and I will keep watch. If anyone comes,

I will wake you in time to scramble to the back of the shed, so don't worry; I will take care of you.

I got my blanket and sneaked all the supplies I thought I would need, and rolled them in my blanket. The hard part was getting a bucket with hot water without being notice.

Mom started the customary ritual to get Ted out of bed, which included cussing, hollering, and her pulling his covers off; it was awful but routine.

That was when I got my bucket of hot water. I set it outside the front door, which was our only door. I ran back into the house and got my blanket. I was set. I even had a roll of gauze in my blanket but no scissors.

Dale was asleep when I got back, and he looked to be in pain. He had his hand holding his side to stop the blood. His hair was streaked with blood.

I did my best and I rinsed him with the cold water from the hose and he shivered.

He yelled, "No!" with the iodine, but I put it on anyway.

I didn't know how to put the gauze on his cut, so I wrapped it around him, it tore easy, and I tied it on. I said, "I am asking Jesus to help you Dale, and take away the pain."

He asked me, "Do you talk to Jesus? Does he answer you? "I talk to Him, and He answers me in my heart. My Uncle Allen says that he puts good thoughts and the answers in my mind, and I think they are my thoughts, but they are really Jesus'. That is how He answers me. Uncle Allen says that if you tell Jesus that you believe He is real, and asks Him to come into your heart, He will come and live inside you. You can talk to Him, and He will talk to your heart and your mind. He helped me learn my timetables."

Dale just kept listening and staring at me. He finally closed his eyes and went to sleep. And I covered him with my blanket.

I washed the bucket out with the hose, and worried how I was going to get the supplies back in the house. I brought the bucket back and set it outside the door.

Ted and my Mom were in a big yelling match and weren't paying any attention to anything but who said what last.

While they were doing that, I got everything back in it's place but my blanket and towel. The towel was so bloody that I thought *I would throw them in the incinerator.*

I went in the kitchen and Mom had made scrapple with sausage in it. She planned on frying eggs for Ted but he wouldn't get out of bed. He just wanted to keep sleeping in between cussing mom out. He wouldn't get up.

We had a toaster. There was no pop up toasters in those days if there was we didn't have one. It was electric. You'd pull the sides down and place bread on both sides of the toaster.

I made two pieces for Dale with oleo and jelly and took a nice helping of scrapple and my glass of milk for him.

He scarfed it down, so I thought he was going to be okay. I was proud of my nursing and thought; *I will be a nurse when I grow up*.

Dale went back to sleep and Mom called me in to eat. I said I ate outside and brought the plate and glass in and prayed that Jesus wouldn't tell her that I lied and all I done. But I thought, *if He does it's okay, Dale is worth a switching.*

I went to check on him and he was gone with the bloody towel but he had left my blanket. I wondered if his Father would whip him again when he got home. I prayed for him and wondered if he went home or was maybe to the pond.

I wanted to find him, but Mom said that there was a section of the yard close to our victory garden that she wanted weeded, and it would take most of the day. I hated weeding, I knew that the section she told me to weed would be done to her satisfaction before I could go anywhere, and that meant done right.

I thought, *"I am going to work so fast and hard that I will get it weeded in time to go down to the pond and be home by 3:00 p.m.*

We had eaten breakfast so late that we wouldn't be eating lunch. I was done by 1:30, took a couple of oranges with me and off to the pond I went.

Dale wasn't there, I ran up by his coop but didn't see or hear anything. *Maybe they took him to the hospital*, I thought.

Walking back I ran into Lillian and she got a haircut for the summer. She told me that the beauty operator had told her not to shave her forehead anymore because the hair would become stiff like a beard. The operator said that when hair grew on the forehead, it meant that you were smarter than other people. I said, "It must be true, Lil, because you are smart and can sing better than anyone in the world."

I have to go, I have to be home by 3:00, see you latter. I got home, and Ted was washing down the side of the shed. He said that he thought a large bird or some animal hit the side of it. There was blood on the side and in the grass, but he couldn't find a dead animal anywhere. It must have flown away.

I went to Tinkers everyday looking for Dale. It was several days before I saw him. He was there buying bread for his mom.

Everything was back to normal, but he thought he might be coming down with the mumps because he had had them before and his jaw felt the same way.

"You can't get the mumps twice unless you only had them on one side" I said. "Hey, Dale, I've got two nickels from my concession work. Do you want some candy?"

"No, my jaw hurts and I don't feel good but thanks, Peggy. You are my best friend."

"Maybe a Coke or a 7 up? My Mother drinks 7 up if she feels squeeze."

"Okay, are you sure?

"Yes".

My neck and jaw hurts real bad, Peggy. Thanks for the 7 Up, I've got to go."

I never saw Dale again. I knew he was sick, but no one knew just how sick. The tetanus bacteria entered his body through the cut on his side, probably caused by the soil contaminated by chicken feces.

The tetanus vaccine was available by 1940 but no one in our area had any vaccinations. We never went to the doctor unless we had a very high fever. We got a smallpox vaccination at school, but other than that, I don't remember any. It is possible I may have received a tetanus shot in Los Angeles, I really don't know.

Dale died and I believed his father had killed him. I grieved uncontrollably. My Mother said, "Enough, move on, he is in heaven." I couldn't move on not yet anyway. He was my secret friend, he was my special friend, and he was my best friend.

CHAPTER TWENTYSIX

I haven't grieved enough or cried enough yet. Don't make me hold my feelings in; they are still set. God gave me my emotions, and I don't mean to cause a commotion. I am not in despair. I believe in God's care, and I know He feels my sorrow, and maybe He will restore my Joy tomorrow. Joy is a fruit of the Spirit, not a right to bring forth by my might. I am experiencing a loss that I can't just toss aside. Please weep by my side.

"Snap out of it, Peggy, You have mourned enough, and now it is time to move on. I want you to get that look off your face, get your skates, and go to the market in town and see if there is any fresh pineapple left. The season is just about over. Ask the produce man to pick out a ripe one for us. If they don't have a fresh one get a medium-size can of sliced pineapple and a pound of brown sugar. Can you carry that much back on your skates? It will go in just one bag."

"Yes, I can".

When you get back, you may help me make an upside-down pineapple cake."

I sucked in my breath. I had never helped Mom make a cake or cook. I had only set the table and made a salad if we had lettuce. I thought, *I am going to skate so fast, that she won't believe I am back so soon. It will be fun, and it will surely make me snap out of it. It hurts so bad to cry inside of my body and put a smile on my face at the same time.*

It was fun making the cake with Mom, and my smile was real. There was no fresh pineapple at the market. I got canned, but Mom was happy,

We read the recipe out of her mother's cookbook. I got to help measure the flower and sugar and make the topping. We didn't have a mixer. Mom beat all the ingredients together by hand. We laughed about using our ration stamp for sugar because Mom had somehow saved an extra one. That made it even more fun to know we wouldn't be out of sugar next month.

After we put the cake in the oven, I started to tell Mom about Dale's father, but before I had a chance, she said, "Peggy, we will be moving in with Aunt Caroline real soon, Ted has been drafted in the Army Air Corps, and we can't stay up here alone without a car."

Rumors, false news and factual news about the war, kept Los Angeles churches full. The cloud of fear filled the city but did not paralyze it.

There were not enough men and women to fill the positions needed. Men and women received larger paychecks, and the building of new homes and construction increased.

The Standard of living improved. Los Angeles boomed, boasting a large percentage of America's war production with aircraft companies and all kinds of industry.

It was the boomtown of boomtowns. The population had grown larger then forty states put together. Restaurants and hamburger joints popped up. People were moving out of the Depression. They were working and buying homes. And yet the homeless, poor, and cheap wine bibbers on Skid Row still increased.

Santa Anita Race tracks, Hollywood Bowl, the LA coliseum– all the large stadiums closed down because of the war. They were used for the war effort and Japanese relocation camps.

Terminal Island in Los Angeles Harbor was under martial law, declared immediately after the attack on Pearl Harbor.

There was a large community of ethnic Japanese on Terminal Island. They were not trusted at all by many other people. The very sight of them created fear and their presence was intolerable to the U.S. military. The government authorities raided the island, rounded up the entire male Japanese first, and shipped them off to an internment camp in Lincoln, Nebraska, because most other interment camps were not ready yet. Soon the women and children where relocated to new interment camps, and the men were joined with them.

There were 120,000 ethnic Japanese evacuated to relocation camps, and over half came from the Los Angeles area. Remember, the Japanese had just bombed the United States, and they had plans throughout the war to bomb our city with seaplanes. We had reason to fear the ethnic Japanese.

I didn't tell Mom that day about Dale's Daddy whipping him with a chicken and that he was hiding in our yard with terrible cuts. I didn't tell -not yet, Mom was consumed with her own problems that day, and she didn't want me moping around.

But most people in our hills knew what Dale and his brothers went through, and Dales daddy was not off the hook. He was in more trouble than he knew.

Mom said, "Tomorrow I want you to say goodbye to all your friends and tell them we will be back after the war. Then we will clean out our victory garden, weed any bad areas, and spruce up the yard.

Dad has given our chickens to Ray and Ida, and Uncle Ray and Uncle Allen are going to keep an eye on the place and not let the weeds become a fire hazard or an eyesore.

I spent that whole day with my friends in the hills, and we cried together about Dale. It was so sad, and we said our goodbyes.

Lillian wanted to talk more about Dale. She said her mother cried and cried and was really upset when Dale died.

She said that Fred, Dale's daddy, might be charged with manslaughter because he made those cuts on Dale by whipping him too hard. They didn't take him to the doctor in time. Their neighbor told my Mother that he could hardly get his breath, and he was having some kind of seizures and got real stiff. His mother came over to the neighbors' for help.

The doctor asked Dale how he gotten so many cuts, and he said, "The chicken did it". He died the next day. That made me cry again. I knew how he had been cut, but I didn't tell Lillian what happened, I just cried and she cried with me.

His oldest brother told the doctor what Dale meant by the chicken cutting him. He himself had many of those whippings, and the doctor took a written report.

"Lillian, what is manslaughter? What does that mean? "I don't know for sure. I think it means beat somebody up."

"I won't be here, Lillian. How will I know what happens?"

I don't know, Peggy. I'll tell you everything when you come home."

My Mother didn't know too much about Fred. If she had, she probably would never have let me explore the hills or let me walk the long way home from school. I decided never to tell her.

Rumor had it that one time his next-door neighbor heard screaming and a commotion coming form their property. He ran over and saw Fred whipping his "Kid" with a live chicken in the chicken coop yard. He realized Fred was drunk and tried to stop hm. Fred told him to get off his property, that it wasn't any of his damn business, that he could correct his kids anyway he saw fit. Fred took a swing at the neighbor and fell flat on his face and his boy ran off.

The next day we worked in the yard as planed. I was doleful and Mom told me to get that look off my face, to get some hustle and bustle going or she was going to give me something to be sad about.

That evening we visited Uncle Ray and Aunt Ida to say our goodbyes. We knew we wouldn't be seeing them until the war was over. They were involved in building their house, and they worked on it seven days a week.

After they expressed their concern for Ted being drafted in the Army Air Force and how they would miss us, the conversation shifted to the Fadner's.

Their lot was close to the Fadner's, so even though they were new in the neighborhood they heard all about what happened to Dale.

Ted and my mother got an ear full about the Fadner family and agreed that Fred had crossed the line and would have to answer for Dale's death. They spent most of the evening taking about it and about Tetanus and the vaccination. Uncle Ray said that he had a close friend who died with it and that they have a horrible death.

Aunt Caroline quit her cooking job, and went to work for North American Aviation plant, and tripled her income. She bought a brand-new home five miles south of Los Angeles.

The city gushed with work and money. Aunt Sadie and Uncle Merle bought a beautiful home five miles S/E of the Los Angeles area and Aunt Sadie went to work for an aircraft plant.

The world's thorny switch was still switching Julian.

Her life and her fate would never enjoy the prosperity of the state she loved so much. She truly was a victim of disguised fear, her undeveloped capabilities, and her dispirited esteem.

We lived with Aunt Caroline and Ralph. Marylou was back home, Howe had joined the Navy, and Henry and Herb were in High school. They were still too young to join the Navy without their Mother's consent, and they were working on that day and night.

Mom went to work with Aunt Caroline, and Grandma took care of Teddy Glenn.

It was Julian's first job other than concession work and she acted as though she had been freed from a painted birdcage, not a gilded one. She loved it, and you would have thought she struck gold with her first paycheck. She probably felt independent for the first time in her life, or she just liked all the hustle and bustle. Whatever-she was a happy lady. We started going to the neighborhood church, and things were good.

Aunt Caroline had an RCA Victor wind up record player, and the kids had all the records they wanted. They had a piano and Herb could play anything on it. It was a happy house accepts for the tension that was always there between Ralph and the boy's.

Henry and Herb were never home during the day that summer. I am not sure what they did. I think they had a paper route. They had bikes and maybe part-time jobs. They were good boys. They were good to me and I loved them.

They both enlisted in the Navy in 1945 with their Mothers signature, although the war was almost over.

Marylou and I had to do the housework in the morning and the two of us fought and yelled at each other every day all through our chores. When the chores were done we went to the park pool and got to stop at Thrifty Drugs for an ice cream.

I don't remember how long we were there that summer before Ted was transferred to Wichita Falls, Texas, A.A.F. base and he wanted Julian to follow him there. Julian quit her job, and we took the train to Wichita Falls Texas.

There were no vacancies in apartments or other housing. The city was filled with military and their families. Ted found a family that rented out their extra bedroom, and he took it.

It was like a boarding house except this was a single-family three-bedroom home. They had two girls that shared a bedroom. Ted, Mom, and Teddy Glenn slept in one bedroom and I slept with the two girls. We had breakfast and dinner with these people. I don't know if they were trying to help the war efforts or how Ted found them. They were real nice and served good food.

We were only there a short time before Ted was transferred to Lincoln, Nebraska, A.A.F. base. My mother and I followed. The situation was the same. The city was filled with military and their families.

Ted found a rooming house. And we had a large bedroom. I had a single bed, Teddy Glenn had a crib, and Ted and Julian had a double bed. We were all in the same room. We had our own bathroom and shared the kitchen, which included a real refrigerator and an icebox. Everyone put their name on the food that belonged to them.

School started in August and I started fifth grade at Prescott Elementary. It was only two blocks from our rooming house, and I walked to it by my self the first day.

The school was very large and had double doors on both sides of the building. When time to go home, I went out the wrong side. The streets looked the same. They were lined with old, beautiful oak trees and large houses that were turned into rooming houses or boarding houses. I was lost.

I walked back to the school, not realizing that there were two sets of double doors, and started again walking down the same street again, thinking I missed our house. I panicked after walking about three or four blocks not finding my house. I didn't know where I was.

Beverly McCoy (Harlow)

I thought, *"Mom will be out looking for me and she won't be able to find me".*

I turned around, and started walking, and saw the school and ran to it all out of breath. This time I went inside. They were just about to lock the doors. The minute I walked in, I saw the other doors and realized what I had done.

I didn't know what time it was, but I thought I was going to get a switching and started to tear up. Mom would think I played after school, and she wouldn't believe I got lost because you could almost see our rooming house from the school. And she had walked me down the day she registered me, and we walked back together.

When I got home, Mama was in bed sick, and Teddy Glenn was not there. A lady who lived in the rooming house saw me come home, and she had Teddy Glenn. She said, "Your mother has been sick all day and has been vomiting. She said that you would be home after school to watch the baby and that her husband would be home too. I have been watching the baby most of the day and waiting for you.

"Oh, thank you" I said.

I took Teddy Glenn and asked Mom what I could do. She said, "Just take care of Teddy Glenn. When Dad get's home, he will fix dinner." She never knew it had gotten so late, and she felt better the next day. I would never want my mother sick. But I can remember being glad that day. I don't think I really thought about her or how she felt. I thought only about myself and how lucky I was that no one knew I was late getting home from school.

I don't remember if Ted got to come home every night from base or periodically, or if he got to stay over night off base at all. I remember the bus was our transportation, and we lived very close to the base.

Almost every night while we were in Nebraska, Ted wanted Mom to come with him to the Canteen on base to relax. He could guzzle beer, which was cheap on the base, and they could dance to live bands. That is the life he enjoyed.

I took care of Teddy Glenn, and sometimes another kid who lived in the rooming house would come visit me and we would play "Fish and "Old Maid". By the time Ted and Mom got home, I was asleep.

Julian had been a Christian since she was a child and married men whom she thought were Christians. She met both of her husbands at church, and they both said that they were believers. Maybe they were, but already had addictions that they could not control.

Julian wanted to live the Christian life. She thought if she would not be fanatical about church and be acting all self-righteous, and is willing to go dancing once in a while, that this would satisfy Ted. Then maybe he would

ALL SWEPT UNDER THE RUG

go to church once in a while, and they could have it both ways.

Julian always left feeling guilty going out night after night leaving her kids home alone to go dancing and drinking to satisfy Ted. Ultimately, She was not willing to live the nightlife that he wanted to live. Soon they were quarreling, and she wanted to go home.

I don't know how the decision was made, but Mom, Teddy Glenn and I were on the train headed for Aunt Sadie, Uncle Merle, and their son Brian's new home. Brian, my cousin, was the same age as Marylou and Pauline.

Aunt Sadie loved Julian more than all her sisters, and she wanted her to come live with them from the beginning. Sadie only had the one boy, and she always worked. Mom wouldn't stay there without paying her fare share, and Caroline really needed her. Julian went to work with Sadie in the air Craft factory; Grandma took care of Teddy Glenn.

CHAPTER TWENTYSEVEN

"Black and white?" No, it's a complex fight. War knows no constraints. The press and propaganda and all that hates try to steal our fate. To die for liberty is our responsibility, but to die for mans ideology should be banned without apology. The nature of goodness was lost at The Fall. Restoration is needed for all.

There has never been anything worst or more violent than the Crucifixion of Christ. There has never been anything greater or better for mankind than the Crucifixion of Christ.

I have never lost my faith. I believe in Christ and that he paid the penalty for my sins. When I was young, why I had to pay for Adam and Eve's sin was a stumbling block for me. I didn't commit their sin. I wasn't even there. I certainly understood my present sins and thought I was on my way to hell more than once before getting on my knees.

When I understood The Fall better, I understood that even Adams sperm was corrupted and that's how he passed the original sin on to me. Everything in the Fallen World is contaminated and is ruled by Satin. It is his world, and, the Bible says we are not to be a part of it. No matter how hard I try not to be part of it, my temperament pulls me into it.

I am convinced that it is only because Christ paid for Adam's (my) original sin, my past sins, my sins today, and my sins for tomorrow, that in God's eyes I am not a part of this Fallen World. God sees me as His kid perfect in Christ, with all my sins forgiven and forgotten. I am part of His Kingdom.

There are many bad things that have happened in our world since the history of man, and I can't name many of them. We seem to forget them soon after they happen unless it happens to us.

I think that is good, we would go crazy if we thought about things like that all the time.

We say, "We should know our history so we don't make the same mistake." I think that who ever said that first started a cliché that sounds so right. Barf. We don't even know for sure when or who discovered America. And most of today's generation know nothing about WW1, WW2, the Korean Conflict, Viet Nam or any war and don't want to. I don't blame them, do you? War is Horror. Anyway, to know doesn't seem to keep us from making the same mistakes, over and over again.

I think the Holocaust should forever be remembered. And of course we remember hearing about other horrors that has happened in our world. Most of us can't put a date to any, but we know some general aspects. Hey, we are from America. We don't worry about any of it. Some call us the "Ugly

Americans," because we seem not to have a care. That is not true Americans do care that's what makes America great.

"Starvation", Maybe that would trigger some questions about a man named Josef Stalin and something about Ukraine. It could, but I hope not to be quizzed about it, or other starvation horrors, such as the big one in China not too long ago. That was just a short time ago wasn't it?

There is something way back when about, "Black Death" Remember that one? No need, I think that is when people believed in witches and that witches all had cats, so they killed all the cats that killed the rats. The rat population enlarged big time and were all infested with fleas, and when a rat died the flees that carried the "Black Death" virus would jump on the people for a nice juicy snack and their bite was 100 percent fatal. Well, that was their silly fault. No need to remember that one, that couldn't happen in America; or could it?

You say that you believe in good witches and bad witches? "Oh my, I don't". "Do the good witches have white cats and the bad witches have black cats? No worries; we have antibiotics so history can't repeat itself. Can it?

There is a world horror that we are all experiencing right now and I don't think we will ever get a chance to forget it and that is, fanatical terrorisms; it is happening to us right now and in America.

We were sitting at the dinner table. Actually we were in the breakfast nook at the table having dinner when we watched Aunt Caroline drive up in front of the house.

She was by herself. We watched her sprint from her car, slamming the door closed at the same time. Hurrying, she stumbled and fell over the curb. Uncle Merle jumped up first, and we all followed, racing out to rescue her. She was crying and we didn't know if she was crying because she hurt herself or something had happened.

Oh, she cried, "I'm not hurt". She was rubbing her knee. The neighbor saw and ran over to help. "I'm okay. I just scrapped my knee a little bit. It's okay. Thank you. Oh shit, I think I need help into the house. Ooh, I can't stand on my foot" She moaned.

Caroline had more than just a skinned knee. She had sprained her ankle. It was a very bad sprain that would take many weeks to heal. She was unable to work and was in a miserable condition.

Uncle Merle and the neighbor man lifted Caroline somehow and got her into the house. She again thanked the neighbor. And it was obvious that she was anxious for him to go home. He said, "If you need me for anything, don't hesitate." Merle thanked him, and he went home.

"Ralph is dead! Caroline blurted. "He was found this morning sitting on a bench, dressed in his brown pin stripped suit and his brown felt hat as though he was waiting for a bus. He was dead. He evidently didn't come home last night. I went to bed early and didn't wait up for him.

The man that found him was a drinking friend of his for years. I know him. His name is Jack. He has been over to the house to visit and also for dinner. In fact, I know him rather well. He's a drunk but a nice man.

"He thinks Ralph was mugged and received a blow that killed him. He is carrying on something awful and claims Ralph was his best friend. He is very upset and shocked. Ralph's eyes bulged, his glasses were knocked off his face, and he was splattered with blood. His noise was blue and twice its normal size. His mouth was open, and his lips were swollen and blue with coagulated blood around his mouth and chin. It looked like he had been sitting there dead for a long time. He was stiff. His hat was on his head, and his head lay back against the bench.

"The police came to notify me this morning and asked me to come down and identify him. It for sure is Ralph. Oh my God he is gone, Julian." Caroline cried. I loved him. He gave me more affection then anyone has in all my life. He never found fault with me or yelled at me, even when I took sides with the boys.

Thank God my two boys are still home with me. I don't think I could face this without my kids, I wish Howe was home. I can't stop worrying about him. What if he gets killed?"

Caroline smoked one cigarette after another and drank black coffee. She had no idea what a hard four weeks she was about to encounter. The only pain she felt right then was anxiety and uncertainty.

She just kept talking, "He didn't have a wallet on him and that's why Jack is sure he was mugged. The police didn't think he was mugged because his clothes were not mussed. But he always carried a wallet in his back pocket.

The only thing he had on him was an almost empty bottle of Jack Daniel in his breast pocket, an open pack of Camels, and a handkerchief. He had no change. He always carried change.

"I am going to make funeral arrangements tomorrow, and I need your help, I can't look at a casket. I don't know where to start. Julian, Ted and Irene need to be notified. Will they let Ted come home for the funeral?"

Merle spoke up, "Caroline, you need to slow down. You can't even stand on your foot. If they think there is foul play, there will be an autopsy. The first thing we need to do is call a funeral director. They take care

ALL SWEPT UNDER THE RUG

of everything. Did Ralph have an insurance policy of any kind?"

"No, but he has social security and some kind of a pension from when he was a tailor," Caroline responded with an uncertain voice and expression.

Merle hesitated, and looked at her with sympathy before he replied, "Okay, lets go back to your house and see if we can find his pension information, get his social security information and pick out a funeral home. Caroline, you know we have to go to work tomorrow, but you can do everything necessary by phone right here. We will get the phone numbers you will need. You stay with us tonight.

Tomorrow, you can find out prices and what you need to work with. Everything is going to fall in place."

"No, Caroline replied. I don't know how to use the phone. We haven't had a phone for years. I wouldn't know what to say she spurted with sincere fear."

"Well Caroline, your first call will be to your work and you won't have any trouble after that, you don't have a choice Sis" Sadie quickly injected.

"Can you make it back out to the car? Asked Merle. Come on Caroline, we will help you through this. We will take off from work to help you if need be, don't worry we are here for you." Merle was doing his best to comfort her.

Sadie said, "We need to pick up Marylou, Caroline. She's going to wonder where you are, and we need to let the boy's know what is going on.

Merle suggested, "Julian, why don't you stay here with the kids and see if you can get through to Ted? Do you have an emergency number for him"?

"Yes, it doesn't go to him, but it goes to his commanding officer. I don't know how to get a hold of Irene. She doesn't have a phone. Oh hell, no one has a phone, what a mess" said Julian.

"Well, if we get back in time this evening, we'll drive over to her house," Sadie said. "You don't need to be getting upset".

Julian answered with anger in her voice, "And you don't need to tell me if I should be upset or not. This happens to be Ted and Irene's father, and I feel an urgent responsibility to notify them immediately. Damn, I have worries too, I can't run out tonight in the dark and take a streetcar to Irene's. I want to get a hold of Irene tonight. She is part of this situation and family too. I am not going to treat her like a second fiddle, like she doesn't have feelings or count. This is her father, Remember?"

Sadie said, "Settle down sis, I didn't mean to make you angry."

Julian continued, "What do you mean, if you get back in time? What time? If you won't drive me up there when you get back I will take a streetcar tonight. And as far as going to work tomorrow, I think the death of my husband's father is reason to stay home and help Caroline with all this phone calling and crap. She will also need help with her foot and be served breakfast, lunch and dinner."

Merle spoke up, "You are right Julian, we all need to slow down and think what we should do. Let's make a list.

"Well, Julian said, if I have to quit my job and move in with Caroline until she can get around, I will. She is going to need help, sis. I am sure my work will consider this an emergency, and I am sure you will be able to do your work tomorrow even if you stay up all night tonight."

Now Caroline was sobbing and rightly feeling sorry for her self, "Oh Julian, thank you, I won't worry if you stay with me. Merle and Sadie, thank you so much for helping me. I don't know what I would do with out you.

Let's don't get into a fight. Let's go. I know where Ralph's papers are. It won't take us long to get what we need. Irene needs to be notified and she might want to come home with us for the feeling of family; I would."

Well it did all work out. There was no autopsy. There would have been if Caroline had insisted, but the detective told her that he thought he had a cerebral hemorrhage, and Caroline seemed satisfied with that. The detective told her that is what a cerebral hemorrhage looked like when they died. He had no real evidence of a beating and his clothes were completely undisturbed.

Jack, Ralph's friend, was horrified and even offended because they wouldn't listen to him. "Just scrape him up and throw him away, I tell you he was mugged. And when they were through, they straighten his clothes and propped him up like a manikin. Did anyone find his wallet?"

Jack came to the funeral, and he cried like a man who had lost his brother. He told Ted what he saw when he found Ralph's body, how long he had known Ralph, and that he knew he was mugged.

I heard Ted tell Julian that he thought Caroline's boys had done it. Julian said, "Look Ted, those are my nephews, and I don't appreciate your accusation. If Caroline would ever here you say such a thing that would be the end of our relationship. He's dead. Lets forget it." They did but, there has always been a question mark.

In about a year, Aunt Caroline met another man to be her husband, Gordon Mottley. They dated about three months and were married. He was so possessive of her that he was even jealous of Marylou and was constantly picking on her. Marylou ran away from home at age fifteen because of it. She and her boy friend eloped to Reno Nevada and got married. They had five children, lost a baby boy but mostly lived happy ever after, serving Christ and never allowed the worlds thorny switch to ruin their life together.

It was fun living with Aunt Sadie and Uncle Merle.

Everyone on their street had a beautiful home and kids of all ages, and we played every game imaginable. Most of the men were in the military, and most of the women worked in factories. Saturday was every ones house cleaning and yard cleaning day. The evenings were for watering, visiting, homework and play right up to bedtime. Sundays were church and picnics at the park. It was my kind of life.

Now it was November, time for my birthday. I received a present from Ted through the mail. It was art supplies: Drawing pad, pencils, water paints, charcoal and colored pencils it was real nice.

But the discussed look that Aunt Sadie gave me only reminded me that she thought I made the story up about Ted.

If I acted like I didn't want the present, I would be an unappreciative brat of all that Ted has done for me, especially when my real daddy hadn't even gotten me a birthday gift. If I acted as though I was thrilled with excitement, that was like an admission that I'd lied about Ted. Of course, the answer was to pretend not to notice Sadie's look or her attitude, just ignore her play dumb, and move on. But I didn't do it this time.

While Aunt Satie and Mom was watching me open this gift, I remembered that Aunt Sadie had said that I had a big imagination about the boy with a pole for a leg who came out of our shed. I said, "Mom, did you tell Aunt Sadie about Dale and what happened to him?"

"No, she didn't, said Aunt Sadie. Who is Dale and what happened to him?"

I know I had the biggest smile on my face when I said, "He was the boy hiding in our shed when you were helping Mom clean."

I was so glad to tell her that I had not made that story up. It was just the perfect time because I know she was thinking about poor Ted and the trouble I caused. And here he was being such a good daddy to remember my birthday, and I wasn't even his kid.

I didn't make any comment on my present. I almost sucked in my checks, but I didn't. I just put my present away and Aunt Sadie was ineffable I felt a satisfaction within. I pray it wasn't revenge.

Be aware, no one escapes the world's thorny switch. One day at her job, Aunt Sadie was working with a drill press with no safety guard. In those days, none was required. This particular day, Sadie was drilling a series of holes in a template. She dropped an item she was working on, and when she bent over to pick it up, her hair got wrapped up in the shaft of the drilling press and scalped her.

Can you imagine anything more painful? She was a long time recovering from that, if she really ever did. Her hair did grow back but she never let it grow long again.

Brian Aunt Sadie's son, was good to me he let me ride his bike and he taught me how to play touch football. He teased me a lot but I teased back as I had private lessons on how to do that from Henry and Herb. It was fun unless he teased me in front of his friends, and that made me melancholy because I felt rejected and hurt. I forever beat him at checkers. He was as bad as Marylou, but he never gave me an Indian burn instead he just pretended that he let me win.

Uncle Merle was always happy and telling jokes. He worked hard, and when he got home from work, he would work in the yard or his garage. He gave Aunt Sadie everything she wanted. They always had a nice home and car.

Sadie kept her house spotless, and was able to buy pretty things to decorate with. She was the first in the family to have a vacuum, and it was a Kirby. She got Venetian blinds, something new on the market. Merle bought her leather purses, shoes, and silk hose. They had many friends and went square dancing, to the roller derby and other sport events.

Uncle Merle was a boxer as a young man. He also attended Angelus Temple Bible College (LIFE) and graduated. That was the same Bible College that Chuck Smith from Calvary Chapel Costa Mesa graduated from. And of course it was at Angelus Temple where Merle meant Sadie.

When the war started, Merle went to work for the railroad, where he learned carpentry on passenger trains.

I would say World War 11, Sadie working in the factories, the Hollywood movies, and their friends got Merle and Sadie to start smoking. That was the fad. Their church believed that all of that was a sin and they backslid as far as being active in the church. They never lost their faith but it was a long time before they got back into church, and when they did, Uncle Merle preached and had much to say.

We lived with Merle and Sadie for four months, maybe a little longer. The war in 1944 was still raging, but when Germany collapsed, we knew we were going to win. The military started bringing men home from Europe.

The war in Japan continued and so many more lives were lost. Even though the Japanese Empire knew they were losing, they refused to surrender and boasted that they that they never would. Finally the United States dropped two atomic bombs, the first one in the city of Hiroshima killing 80,000 people not counting the ones who died of radiation poison. The second atomic Bomb was dropped on the city of Nagasaki, killing

40,000, again not counting the ones who died of radiation poisoning. The Japanese surrendered in the next day or so.

Speculation has it that if those bombs had not been dropped, a million or more American and Japanese soldiers would have been killed.

The war with Japan was not declared over until September 1945. Ted had been discharged much earlier, and we returned home.

CHAPTER TWENTY-EIGHT

Everyone has a home. It's a place that we find in our mind. It is not any dwelling made of wood with walls, floors, and goods. It's not a tent made out of lent or a coop, a cave, a trailer, or a ship made for a sailor. For some it is only an imagination that comes because they have never had a real one. A home can be memories good and bad with consequence that make us sad and glad. My home is the peace that God placed in my heart as I needed Him desperately right from the start.

I recognized the faint smell of the cesspools as we turned the corner for our coop. But instead of letting that penetrate I imagined the smell of the fresh, wild, dark green grass that grew all over my hills.

I thought of the pollywog pond divided by a rock mound, from our own private pool.

I wondered about Dales daddy, and Lillian, and all my Arkie family. And then a strange, ridiculous thought that wasn't very nice entered my mind just as we drove up to our coop.

I thought, *we should have dug up Aunt Sadie's house and hooked it on a big truck and brought it to our lot. We would dig up our coop and give it to Aunt Sadie.* And then I thought how funny our coop would look on Aunt Sadie's street and I started giggling.

Mom said, "What are you giggling about?"
"I don't know. I just can't stop."

I think that was the day that my giggles developed.

All girls have them you know. I never got control of my giggles until I was seventeen. I still have them, but I learned to control them because most adults think you are silly or you are an airhead if you giggle.

I do care what other people think even though I think there is a cliché that say's we shouldn't care I do care. I like people and I like being accepted, and that gives me the most sanguine personality.

I thought, *here we are, I am so anxious to get in touch with everyone, but I mustn't let on. I won't act anxious or for sure they won't let me go. I'll just be quiet and help unpack and take care of Teddy Glenn for Mom and Ted.*

Teddy Glenn is three years old now, and he was so cute. I was teaching him his colors and he is stuck on the color yellow. He really had to be watched closely now because he got into everything, ran everywhere, and he didn't like to hear the word no. He wanted me to play with him all his waking hours he didn't like to play alone.

One time we were visiting Aunt Virginia, and Teddy Glenn said, "Me a cookie, An Genga." He was about two years old.

Mom playing with him, picked him up, and said, "You are not supposed to ask." She ruffled his tummy and hair and kissed him all over. She thought it was so cute.

Aunt Virginia said, "Oh Julian, he can ask Aunt Virginia for anything."

It wasn't long after that we visited Grandma Dorsey, and Teddy Glenn said, "Gamma I smell cookies". He was the baby of the family, and all claimed him. We spoiled him rotten, but he never got into trouble growing up.

It took three days to settle back into our coop counting grocery shopping. Mom changed all the sheets and washed all the dishes in the cupboard, and I dried dishes while Teddy Glenn napped.

My main job was to take care of Teddy Glenn, and he was a handful. I was not free to leave the house for three anxiety filled days.

Smog may have always been in California. I don't know and would never debate the issue. I have heard it called seasonal, but we never experienced any smog that we were aware of until 1947.

Can you even imagine the valley, hills, mountains, and seaside in Sothern California crystal clear, all accessible and open for your convenience, so clear that you could see Catalina from over fifty miles away?

My hills were incredibly different from the city of Los Angeles. And few people have lived only eight miles away from the City Hall in one of the largest cities in America with clear air, clean cold water, and have every kind of fruit tree imaginable and berries everywhere for free picking.

When they were in season, I ate apricots, plumbs, and every different kind of peach, avocados, cherries, and loquats. I don't know what happened to the loquats, which I think, originate from China. Loquats were one of my favorite fruits. It seems as though they just disappeared. Maybe the smog killed them. Canned loquats and the ones they serve in Chinese restaurants taste nothing like loquats picked from the tree.

My, it was a different culture, with the same evil, the same rotten people, and the same descent people. People are people everywhere in a Fallen World, but I think that good and evil are expressed differently in different dispensations (periods of time) For example; we never locked our front door. No one did. We all had the same skeleton key anyway. Camping gear such as camp stoves, fishing poles, things left in your campsite were all safe to leave unguarded.

The first evening we were home, I went out on the patio and was looking up at the sky. There were so many bright stars twinkling. It was stunning against the black space, even for a ten year-old. I wondered how anyone could know for sure if they saw the first falling star at night, and I wondered where it would fall. Did God catch it before it fell to the ground? Could it fall on someone? I was in deep thought.

Ted said, "What are you looking at?" He startled me. I hadn't heard him come out. He was drinking a beer and smoking a cigarette.

"Nothing, "I replied and dismounted the three stairs off the patio to go in the house.

Ted said, "Wait a minute, I want to talk to you."

I said, "No," and I ran in the house. I knew the game would continue.

Mom was still trying to organize our belongings into the three rooms and the bathroom, which really helped. She put our linens in a marked box up against the wall by Teddy Glenn's crib. He had to stay in the crib until they bought a new bed for him. She put a few towels and wash clothes in a small cabinet that sort of fit against the bathroom wall by the door. She put the extra towels and wash clothes in with the linens.

Mom was tired and suggested going out to eat, maybe a sandwich or a breakfast. We went to Thrifty Drugs restaurant, it was really close to the house, and they served breakfast, liver and onions, pot roast, sandwiches, including hamburgers and fries. We ordered hamburgers with fries. Mom and Ted drank coffee, and I got a fountain cherry coke that was very special. We shared everything, including my cherry coke with Teddy Glenn.

Mom and Ted talked about getting back in concession right away. Mom had saved all her checks from her jobs, and Ted got a mustering out check when he was discharged. They had enough money to take the time necessary to get back into the business. Mom mentioned the large room to be built off the kitchen. It was a nice evening, and we all rested up.

We had been invited to Ray and Ida's for dinner the next night. And I was anxious because I knew their conversation would be about the Fadner's and I wouldn't have to ask any questions.

We were surprised to see the house it was nice, and they were so proud of it. They had a living room, bedroom, kitchen, and bath downstairs, two bedrooms and a bath upstairs. They had bought two lots together and were doing a lot of cement work. They poured a patio, and planters. They planted a large victory garden, baby fruit trees and never-ending ideas for their yard.

Finally the real conversation began. Dale's Father had been arrested for possible murder and did not have bail money, so he stayed in jail until they had a trial. They found him guilty of child endangerment and manslaughter, and he was sentenced to six years in California State Prison. I wondered what bail money and manslaughter were, but I didn't ask. I was already tearing up. I would wait and ask Lil.

Aunt Ida said that the Fadner place was empty. Someone had burned down the chicken coop. someone was taking care of the property, but didn't know who. She thought the family had moved away with Mrs. Fadner's relatives.

The neighborhood had organized a memorial-type gathering for Dale and invited us to go but we felt that we didn't know the family and we would be strangers showing up to watch everyone else mourn, so we didn't go.

Then Aunt Ida said to me, "I understand that you will be going to junior high in September. Did you know that Bobby, Irene's oldest boy, will be attending the same school with you in September?"

"No, where will Larry and Jimmy be?

Ida said that they would be staying with their father that Bobby will be living with us permanently. Larry might live with his father's sister. Their father was sick and having a hard time of it.

Ted's uncle Ray was his mother's brother, and Irene, being his niece, felt that he and Ida could raise one of the boy's but were to old take on all three. Maryann, their daughter, was still home, and the house would be too small for three boys and a grown daughter. Irene and Jane, her daughter lived with her mother in an apartment, and there was no room for her boys.

All three of the boys were going to stay with us for the rest of the summer. Ted pitched an army tent in the front part of our yard.

Bobby was one year ahead of me in school. Larry was in the same grade, and Jimmy would be in fourth grade. Bobby knew he would be living with Ray and Ida and he didn't express much feeling about it. None

ALL SWEPT UNDER THE RUG

of the boys seemed to even think about their fate for the next year.

One more day and I will be free to visit my friends. This last day, we all went grocery shopping together. We got a lot of groceries. Mom said that we needed stables as well as the weekly supply.

We went to Thrifty drugs and replenished our medicine cabinet with aspirin, iodine and gauze, tape-all that is needed for home care. We were ready to take up where we left off.

Mom made a big dinner, and after the dishes were done I wanted to go outside. It was so cool and beautiful, but unless Mom went with me, I was afraid to go out by myself because I knew Ted would follow.

I stayed in and we listened on our radio to *Superman, Inner sanctum, the top Ten Hit Parade* sponsored by Lucky Strike cigarettes, and of course *Swing* with the Big Bands.

Beverly McCoy (Harlow)

"Manslaughter means you killed someone but didn't mean to, and I don't know what bail is" Lil told me. We were so happy to see each other. She told be about everyone and that Dorothy the Dot won top place for the student of 5th. Grade. She told me about this one and that one, and we laughed.

We walked to Tinker's, her Mom gave us a nickel apiece, and we bought penny canny so it would last. We walked down to the pond, and I felt at home at that moment.

We had a fun summer. Ted and Julian lined up concession work for the winter as they planed on taking most of the summer off so as to take the boys. They took a few events but not many.

Bobby, Larry and Jimmy stayed with us and slept in the tent for six weeks. Much of that time was at the beach. Ted wanted to give them a lifetime of fun in those six weeks that they would never forget. Their mother and Jane, Irene's daughter was with us most of that time so as to be with her sons. Irene and Jane slept in the living room with me. Irene slept on the couch and Jane shared my bed. It was fun.

Ted stayed on his best behavior. He drank his beer but he never bothered me. There was no place for him to stay up all night, so he went to bed when everyone else did and got up in the morning instead of the afternoon.

We got our chores done early and were free to drive to Big Bear or maybe to the Brea Tar Pits or the Los Angeles Museum.

We usually brought our food with us but some times Irene chipped in and we would stop for hamburgers, fries, and a coke. Mom always brought a bag full of oranges, raw carrots and soda crackers so if anyone said they were hungry, she would give them an orange, a raw carrot, or a cracker-their choice.

Six kids and three adults can consume a lot of food in a day. Chicken was cheap, most people that lived in the hills raised their own chickens, but we didn't have any that summer. We still ate a lot of fried chicken and beans and more beans and more beans cooked in salt pork. Delicious.

We took our lunch with us on our trips. Ted, my mother, and Irene holding Jane on her lap in the front seat; Teddy Glenn, Bobby, Larry, Jimmy and I rode in the back of the van with all of our food, water, Ted's beer, and what ever we might need for the day.

As long as Ted had beer to drink, a place to go, and something to do, he was happy and pleasant. He would sing songs, try to imitate Bing Crosby, make everyone laugh, and tell jokes. He seldom got tired; his tired time was in the morning.

It was fun to go to Big Bear because Ted would make two or three stops by the streams that flow along the way from Big Bear Lake.

We would climb over the rocks and walk in the stream.

Big Bear was the first recreational mountain in Southern California, and some have the opinion that it is unsurpassed in mountain beauty with it's towering pines and streams that flow down the hill sides from the lake. Every activity can be found there. There was natural hot springs, trout fishing, camping, swimming, hiking, carpenter red ants the size of houses (just kidding, but they are big), country clubs for the rich, and Hollywood hangouts.

Ted told us stories about Big Bear, the Serrano Indians who once lived there, and grizzly bears and how dangerous they were.

It was noted as a filming location, familiar films such as *Gone With The Wind*, a number of *Bonanza* episodes, and many, many others. Mom and I did not like to camp there because of the carpenter ants. In the winter, it was open for all the winter sports to include snowball fights and an incredible change of scenery and weather just a hop, skip, and a jump from the city of San Bernardino.

Big Bear was a small city in San Bernardino County. It was less than 100 miles from our coop but an all-day trip. It usually meant not getting home before 9:00 or 10:00 p.m. with all of us kids asleep. We played hard and long.

Of course, we didn't go somewhere everyday, but we went often. Between the rolling hills, the pond, and our outings, the summer seemed to be gone before it started.

One of those summer days, Aunt Irene and Ted stayed home and took care of the kids all but me. Aunt Ida, my Mother and I went shopping for material and patterns. Aunt Ida had offered to make me some dresses for school. She loved to sew. We had a fantastic day and had lunch at Thrifty Drugs.

Aunt Ida could sew beautifully, and the dresses didn't look homemade. With Pauline's out grown clothes and the dresses that Aunt Ida made for me, I was the best-dressed girl in sixth grade, all but my ugly brown oxfords.

Bobby started seventh grade in style living with Ted's uncle Ray and Ida. He had his own room and they treated him as though he was their son.

Maryann's Mother, Joan, had died of cancer when she was ten, and Ray married Ida May when Maryann turned twelve.

Ida had never been married before. Ray was much older, but the three of them were a good match. Maryann was a daddy's girl, and he and Ida showered her with all she wanted. Ida made clothes for her, and they had a good relationship.

Maryann was a collector. She got a stuffed animal ever year for Easter, and she had saved every one of them. When Bobby came to live with them, she was a grown woman collecting Roosevelt dimes and had a jar full of them.

Bobby was not easy. He wouldn't come right home after school. He was terribly disrespectable to Maryann, treating her as though she too was a child.

Ray had to speak to him unkindly. This was totally against his temperament. He hardly raised his voice.

Bobby started stealing Maryann's dimes one or two at a time at first and then more. He had to go into her room to steal them. She noticed the disappearance, so she hid in her room and caught him.

Ray told Bobby that he called his father and that he was on his way to pick him up. Ray and Ida felt as though they failed him and couldn't trust that he wouldn't continue down this path. They decided that he would be more contented with his father and brothers.

I saw Bobby only twice saw after that, once shortly after he was shot and once just before he died.

CHAPTER TWENTY-NINE

Kindergarten I was boss; sixth grade I was at a loss. I found out I wasn't so smart and didn't even have talent to start. Some boys and girls could sing, tap, and swing. Some could play the piano and dazzle a crowd playing classical. Some won spelling bees knowing all the rules while their mother and father taught them vocabulary clues. Some has artistic ability that was modernistic or realistic. Oh I don't fit. I am a mess compared to the rest.

I was eleven years old and Miss Wooster was my homeroom sixth grade teacher. We never changed classes accept for social studies and physical education. There were only three kids out of forty in my homeroom class that I knew. Dotty the

Dot was one but her mother did not want her to associate with me because I lived in those Arkie and Okie hills where bad things happened and the people lived in dumps and were uneducated and ignorant.

I knew Dottie liked me and we teamed up together for relays in physical education. She will always be my friend because I liked her too. She did well in every subject, to include physical education.

Dot was like me in that she did not have any talents to share, but she encouraged those who did and made new friends quickly. She had eleven brothers and sisters, and like the Dorsey family, they all looked alike. Against her mothers wishes, we were friends.

Chartreuse was not new to the French and had been around for a long time, but it was certainly new to my sixth grade class. Green, yellow, and pink chartreuse full skirts and tops started showing up and were the desire of all. It was to die for, and many of us just had to die. I was one of those. The white oxford shoe became popular, and my mother said that that was ridiculous.

Pretty dresses, tops, and skirts with ugly brown, scuffed Oxford shoes with rubber bands holding the sole to the top of my shoe was my attire in sixth through eight grade.

Except for my shoes, I was proud of my clothes, and knew I was lucky to have them. Aunt Virginia's daughter Pauline had the best of everything, and I got to inherit all her clothes, which were always like new.

It was this year, when I was eleven, that my real father and stepmother had a new baby boy. I got to visit and see my new baby brother, Richard Dean, and my sister Sarah Jean. This would be the last time I would see my sister and baby brother until I was in my 50's because my father and his wife Margie divorced and they disappeared from my life, I could not find them.

Beverly McCoy (Harlow)

There was a new girl in my sixth grade class today and she was pretty with natural curly hair and large blue eyes. She was in the classroom before I got there and was sitting one row over directly across from me. I smiled at her to let her know I wanted to be friendly. She looked at me but didn't smile back.

When the recess bell rang and she got up, I saw that her right leg was much shorter then her left, and when she took a step, it caused her whole left side to drop to the level of her right leg. She had a prominent limp. People want to look at something like that, though most don't mean to stare. It's hard to look without being noticed. It made me think of Dale.

I said, "Hi my name is Peggy. Do you want to have recess with me? She smiled and said, "Okay." I saw that her front teeth were streaked brown. She said, "My name is Susan, and we moved here this summer from

ALL SWEPT UNDER THE RUG

Texas. I have a sister who is six. She just had an operation to remove a tumor, and it has left her blind. That's why I am late starting school. I've been helping at home. Everyone is sad. She is so sick that my Mother seldom leaves her side.

"Oh I am so sorry, Susan. I will pray for her."

"Thank You" she said.

"Susan, what is a tumor?

"My mom and dad say it is like a bump that just keeps growing. My sister's name is Sally, and my daddy says that her tumor was caused by fluoride in our drinking water. That's why my leg quit growing and my teeth have brown streaks. They tried to sue the city, but the city says that fluoride wasn't the cause.

There have been a lot of people in our area-Texas I mean– that have stained teeth. They're the same color as mine, and they have trouble with their bones. There's a big group of people back yonder that is fighting to have the fluoride removed from the water.

"When I am thirteen, I will have an operation in the Children's hospital to make my leg longer. I have to be at least thirteen so I won't' grow any more."

Susan invited me to stay over night with her come Friday and spend the day Saturday. My Mother said that she would have to meet her parents first.

Mom and Ted with Teddy Glenn and me drove over to meet the Wilson's. They lived a little over a mile from our coop in an older large house, something like Caroline's old house. It was close to the same Blvd our junior high school was on. It was close to a main highway leading west out of our area.

The Wilsons were very friendly. Mom said she had a rule that she had to meet the parents of her daughter's girlfriends before she could stay over night.

They said that they hoped they passed the inspection.

Julian felt a little embarrassed that she had been so blunt. But they brushed off the thoughtless statement and offered coffee, beer or wine.

Julian took coffee. Ted thanked him for a beer. Nora Wilson had a glass of wine, and Stan Wilson opened another bottle of beer for himself. He offered us kids milk and cookies.

The Parents acted, as they had known each other for years. Then Mrs. Wilson introduced us to Sally, who was recovering from her surgery and sitting up in her bed with her doll listening to music.

My mother talked to her and hugged her tight with tears coming down her cheeks, Nora cried quietly too. Mom asked if she could pray for her, and Nora said," please do.

My mother prayed for her, and it was very spiritual and sincere. Ted, Stan, Nora, Susan and I joined in the prayer. Before Mom was through, Nora also prayed allowed and then Stan did. The prayers were not said in a sad or scary way for Sally to hear but they were encouraging with a happy tone for her benefit.

Stan said that they would bring me home Saturday evening after dinner. Good, that would be fine. They had to work and wouldn't be home before 8:00 p.m.

We stayed in Sally's room and talked with her for a while, and then we adjourned to the kitchen. Mom had more coffee, Nora had nothing, and Ted and Stan had another beer.

Stan turned the conversation into the water fluoridation controversy. What he mostly had to say came from angry feelings. He knew all the negatives about fluoride and blamed it as the cause for Sally's tumor and Susan's stained teeth, and the fact that her leg quit growing. Nothing or no one could convince him different.

Suzan and I went outside. Our parents talked for a long time before we went home.

I was hoping that Ted didn't drink to much beer and spoil everything.

On the way home Ted and Mom expressed that the Wilsons were really nice people, and she was going to have them over for dinner soon.

Ted didn't know much about fluoridation and listened with interest. He said that Stan made sense. There were too many in their area that has been affected with similar symptoms. There has not been proper testing, and it was not likely Texas was going to take any responsibility for it. There were some reviewers that have insisted that water fluoridation reduces cavities in children's teeth and that it had other unclear benefits.

There had been court cases for a number of illnesses that they believe were caused by fluoridation from the city water supply. So far none have won. The courts favor the cities decision and wouldn't listen. It had turned out to be a political, moral, and economic unsolved problem. The cities started controlling the amount of fluoride levels and that was good. The debate continues today about the amount of fluoride that should be in water. We don't hear too much about fluoride anymore, but this is an interesting reference to read. (The Plutonium Files, W.W.W. Fluoride Alert. Org.)

Susan couldn't do to many physical things. She could walk to the movies from her house and that is what we did Saturday. We saw Shirley Temple and Roy Rogers, two good ones, with two cartoons.

Mom gave me nine cents for the movie and a nickel to spend I was to bring home the penny change. I had some of my own change from my stash that was building up again. Susan and I ate candy through both features.

There was nothing to do when the movies were over. Susan couldn't play hopscotch, catch, or any active games. Paper doll were not fun anymore they were for babies and we were in Junior High now.

We giggled a lot and played with Sally as best we could. She was six years old and could talk quite well, so we tried to play a game, but she was miserable and bitter because she couldn't see anymore. It was too sad to play with her.

We got Sally to stand by her bed and count steps to the bathroom, but she didn't like that. She wanted only to sit because she was afraid she would bump into something and fall. We walked her out on the front porch and she just kept swatting at the air. She could hear all the sounds and couldn't see it was awful.

Susan didn't have any friends at school, she was new, and no one knew how to include her because of her limp. She was not a quiet person but at school she hardly said a word and didn't get acquainted with anyone.

I was still very physical. I still liked to climb trees, skate, and play boys basketball.

In sixth grade the girls had to play nine-court basketball, and it was ridiculous. I liked to play catch with a hardball and mitt, play kick the can and on and on. I was a healthy tomboy.

I felt guilty but I just couldn't be with Susan all the time because it went against my temperament. I seem to understand that she needed me, and I tried hard to take care of her so she would be happy and feel accepted. I hated not to be accepted. I knew the feeling because my aunts and uncles did not accept me. I was always nice to Susan, and I walked over to her house after school now and then.

Slowly I gave way to my own desires, and we gradually were just distant friends. I told her that the summer she got her operation for her leg, I would come and sit with her everyday that I could.

She got that operation at the end of eight grades. She had a full-body cast with both arms free and one leg. She laid on her back in that cast for three straight months. I kept my promise and visited her for two or three hours at a time. The surgery did not lengthen her leg. It was a complete failure.

I was lonely too in this big old school. I didn't fit in. I hadn't grown an inch since fourth grade, my chest was flat, and I was skinny and all feet. Everyone looked at those ugly brown oxford shoes. Some girls had breast and already started their periods. I couldn't sing, or dance or draw. Girls in sixth grade didn't fight anymore so I couldn't even do that. I was a mess.

One time when I got a new pair of shoes and was happy that my feet were growing, Aunt Irene told me that I would one day wish I had small feet; she was so right.

I had to go to work with Ted this Saturday. Teddy Glen was sick, Mom had to stay home with him, and Ted needed help. I helped load the van and off we went to some event that was an all-day affair.

On the way he reached over with his right hand pressed down on my upper leg and said, "We are finally alone. I love you Peggy."

I screamed at the top of my lungs, He said, "Shut up" I wouldn't and I went crazy. He said, "You are going to cause an accident, shut up." I wouldn't.

I don't know if I was that much out of control or I was being theatrical like my Mother. I truly don't know. I felt a power, and I continued. I rolled down the window, and stuck my head out, and started screaming. Ted grabbed me hard with one hand and pulled to the side of the road. He slapped me and said, "Stop it!"

I said, "I won't and I am going to tell everyone at your work. I am eleven years old now and my Mother will believe me. We are going to take Teddy Glen and move far away from you. I said, "I don't want to call you Daddy anymore. You are not my daddy. My daddy wouldn't do that to me."

He said, "You listen to me. You are not going to do any such thing because if you do, I will wipe out this family for good. I will not hesitate to kill your mother, you and Teddy Glen, and don't think I won't. You are going to go to work and help me, and that is all there is to it."

I shut up. We went to the event, and I was quiet. He told me to touch the machine when he plugged it in, and I had one more surge of power. I told him to do it himself because I wouldn't. I did nothing for him but sit on a stool and stare into space. He never said a word to me. I think he was afraid that I would go crazy again. He did not have one beer, and he took care of everything. I did absolutely nothing.

It was a long time before Ted came after me again. I know it is common for girls to go through such experiences. I know it is common that when it happens, the child is usually penetrated and hurt physically as well as mentally.

In any case, it is an enormous burden for a child, girl or boy, and it most always destroys family relationships. Time marches on and life continues.

I walked to my Four Square Church on Pain St. Ted and Julian didn't attend. If I didn't have to go to an event, I walked to Sunday school and stayed for Church. Sometimes Pastor Zelmer and Sister Zelmer would take me home with them so I could go to the evening service. I was very young when I asked Jesus into my heart and talked to Him. However, I was eleven before I really understood.

Someone from the Church picked me up for Wednesday night and choir practice. Pastor Zelmer and Sister Zelmer were the greatest. They had three children but they were older. I was too young to belong to their youth program and to old to belong to the other programs for children.

So Pastor Zelmer and Sister Zelmer would see to it that I got to go with their youngest daughter's youth program. She was three years older but didn't resent me going with her. She was boy crazy, and I never teased or interfered; I just acted nonchalant. I attended the foursquare church on Pine St. by myself from the time I was nine years old until we moved from the area. I was eleven when I asked Jesus to come into my heart with understanding. And though my teenage years were unruly, I never lost my faith.

Sixth grade was my worse year and my best year. I believe that God knew that I needed someone special in my life right then, a certain type of girl with a lot in common. Not too many negatives, on the contrary, all giggle, positive, and never too serious.

Miss Wooster, my homeroom teacher, took the roll, and wrote an assignment in arithmetic on the board. She then addressed the class; "We are going to receive a new girl this morning. Peggy, would you like to be her guide for the week"?

Oh, I almost fell off the chair. "Yes, I replied."

Well, go get her; she is at the office waiting.

I walked to the office, and there stood this skinny little girl with curly brown hair, common blue eyes, a flat chest supporting a pretty dress with ugly brown Oxfords.

I smiled, but she had a smile on her face that was bigger than she was. Her mother was with her and Ann turned to her and said, "Goodbye" and followed me to class.

CHAPTER THIRTY

Time could just be a perspective or a portion of a whole, and that would explain our distortion of how we grow. It takes a whole lifetime to live our first year. And we don't remember a thing; it must have all been a fling. To die at birth or live on earth is God's decision of what dimension, but we will live and never die, so don't you cry. Enjoy the present; that's our lifetime there is no past so live and laugh. Look to the future with God for a task.

I finally quit revealing my crimes to my mom and became quite sneaky at times. I was not one to lie. I was accused of lying about Ted, and I always worried that my Mother thought I was a liar. I am not saying I never told a lie-every one has-but it certainly is not one of my proclivities. To be thought of as a liar with a big imagination about such a thing hurt more than the verbal and (fondling) sex abuse. I never wanted to get caught in a lie because that for sure would prove I lied about Ted, so I don't think I told any deliberate lies.

Sneaking is certainly a form of lying but I didn't think of it that way when I was eleven. My new friend Ann and I would sneak our Mothers lipstick and apply it before school. We were not allowed to wear lipstick because our parents said that we were too young. There were some girls at our school that wore it, so we thought we were not to young. If we would have known words like cool, or sexy, we would have said, "It made us look cool."

Ann and I for sure were not perfect little girls. We usually went to the Saturday matinee if I did not have to go to a concession event. If I got to stay home, Mom gave me quite a few chores, and then it was assumed that Ann and I would go to the movies. Mom would leave a quarter for me. The movies now cost thirteen cents and she let me have the rest for spending. She did not have a clue about my stash.

Ann's family was from Canada. They first settled in Detroit Michigan, but Ann suffered from serious bronchitis and she almost died. Their doctor told them they needed to move to Southern California. He said that he had realities that lived in a particular small city there, and it was dry nearly all year and thought that would be the answer for Ann.

Ann's father was able to transfer his employment. They bought a real cute two-bedroom small home in my skating vicinity. She had a little brother that was the same age as Teddy Glen. We were instant best friends that had so much in common.

Ann had heard about Olvera St and she wanted to know if I ever seen it. I said, "Sure,

It's close to where I used to live. We go to Philippi's, Home of the French Dip, right across the street from there. Ted say's that Olvera St is the oldest street in Los Angeles, so it must be thousands and thousands of years old."

Ann wanted to see Los Angeles and Olvera Street. I said, "Well, maybe Ted and my Mother will take us there and we can get some Mexican food. That is what they make on that street.

And then I got an idea. "Why don't we take the bus down there instead of going to the show? I thought I could take two dollars from my stash, One for Ann and one for me.

Ann was thrilled with the idea. We waited at the bus stop for a bus that said "Los Angeles". I told the driver we wanted to go to Olvera St. and he let us off on the closes street on his route to Olvera St. We got off the bus giggling and as carefree as we could be.

I thought the bus went right to Olvera St. and we would just be there. I didn't know my way around the city of Los Angeles. I didn't know the street that the bus driver let us off on. I didn't know where I was or how to find Olvera St. I was lost. I started to panic but I didn't want Ann to know I was lost and pretended to know where I was. I thought, *if I saw someone on the street I would ask how to get to Olvera St.*

We walked and we walked. Pretty soon I fessed up. Ann just giggled she or I didn't realized the danger I put us in.

There wasn't any one walking around where we were and no stores. Finally we saw a bus bench and waited for a bus that went back to our city. Three or four busses went by but not for our city.

Maybe we could take a taxi, I thought. I saw one go by. We were hungry, and there was no place to eat. We saw a couple of bums on the street but were afraid to talk to them.

Beverly McCoy (Harlow)

Now I was getting scarred, and I said, "Ann, what are we going to do?"

Ann's parents had a phone and Ann said, "I can call my parents, but they will be so angry that I probably will never get to be friends with you again."

I said, "If my mother finds out, I will never be trusted again."

Mom quit switching me so much that year because I was in Junior High, and she said that if I didn't know right from wrong by then, I never would, and I would grow up to be just like my Aunt Betsy. I thought, *I must be like her already.* I got a few switching's but I deserved them just like I deserved one now.

I said, "Oh Ann they can't find out. There is still time. Let's turn on the next street and see what's there." There was a Café– beer joint and we walked in and the bar tender yelled at us to get out. We ran out, and we weren't giggling. There was a yellow Taxi sitting at the curb. I ran to it and told the driver that we were lost. We just wanted to catch the bus to our community unless he could take us.

He laughed, "It cost a lot of money to take you that faraway. Will your parents pay me? I said, "We have two dollars." He said, "No, that is not near enough and he pointed to another cross St. and told us that he thought there would be a bus we could take from there.

We waited, and buses passed but not with the name of our city on them. Finally one came. The driver opened the door even though no one was waiting but us. I told him where we wanted to go and he said that we had to transfer.

"What do you mean?" I asked.

"Well, get on, and I will drop you off where you catch the bus that will take you where you want to go."

That finished our show money, but I had the two dollars, so we had plenty of money to ride the bus home and get a hamburger and an ice cream at our Thrifty Drugs.

Beverly McCoy (Harlow)

We got home early enough that neither her parents nor mine asked questions. I was glad that mine didn't ask me what I saw at the movies. If they had, I wonder if I would have lied? Preteens are a handful and are as vulnerable as the two year-olds in many respects.

At the dinner table that night, "I asked if Ann could go with us the next time we went to Philippi's, Home of the French Dip. Ann wants to see Olvera Street. I told her that we went to Philippe's and that was right across the street from Olvera St." Ted said, "That would be fun. We are free from work tomorrow, and could go tomorrow afternoon. What do you think, Julian? We could stop by and see my mother and sister while we're there.

I think I had a tinge of guilt about trying to find Olvera Street on my own. My face felt hot, and I never said another word during dinner. After dinner and the dishes were done I skated over to Ann's house and ask her if she could go.

She giggled sheepishly asking her parents, and they said yes. She looked at me and said, "Oh my gosh Peggy", and put her hand over her mouth, and I hurried home before it got dark.

Ted had his usual huge breakfast late Sunday morning, and Ann was at my house ready to go by 10:00 a.m. She had breakfast, but she ate some more with us. Good thing because we went to Olvera St. first and looked at everything. Ted loved telling us all the city's historical background.

The first thing Ted did was to buy us each a straw sombrero, including one for Teddy Glen. They were fifty cents apiece we wore them and thought we looked Mexican.

I think Ted and Mom done real well at their concession event Saturday because they were in such a good mood, and they didn't act as though they were on a budget.

Olvera St has a large rubber tree right in front of the entrance. It is so large that it shades the block-long street. The street is a little Mexican marketplace that represents the birthplace of Los Angeles. Vendors are everywhere, as well as old structures, painted walls, cafes, restaurants that serve Mexican food, and gift shops. The smell of tacos, burritos, tamales, and taquitos saturate the air.

Ted and my Mother love Mexican food but they got sick one time and blamed it from something they ate there so they won't eat any Mexican food on Olvera St. They preferred to eat at Philippe's, and in fact considered Philippe's a favorite restaurant.

Most everything is outside, so there were a lot of flies, pigeons, garbage cans, and people from around the world, as well as dirty baby diapers dropped on the ground, bottles, and strollers.

Mariachi music and dancers dominated the sound within this one-block street. The women were dressed in colorful red and green full skirts with peasant blouses, and the men in mariachi costumes with big sombrero felt hats, singing, playing guitars, and dancing.

The merchants sold handcrafted items- leather purse; belts; huaraches; Mexican wooden toys such as jumping beans, Jacob's ladders, and spinning tops; and much more-all from Mexico, all on display seven days a week.

Ann was not disappointed. And her parents had given her some money to spend, and she bought them matching leather chain purses with it.

We were so hungry that we left our amazing street about 4:00 P.M. in the afternoon and went to Philippe's an unusual place in that day and age.

A Frenchman established it in 1908 and he claimed to have created the French Dip. He sold the restaurant in 1927 for five thousand dollars. The man who bought it left it open twenty-four hours a day during the

Depression and during World War 11. It is a landmark today.

The floors are covered with sawdust and there are long tables that you take your food to on trays. All the food is already cooked and ready to serve.

There are probably six or seven lines, each with a serving lady. Everyone eats at the same tables, and there are many tables. People from around the world dine there, to include homeless people and the wealthiest.

The menu is incredible as everything is fixed to perfection. The French dips are made from roast beef, pork, lamb, turkey or ham. Philippe's is also noted for their pickled pigs feet, hard-boiled eggs pickled in beet juice and spices, and yes, and their famous beef stew that they feed to the homeless real cheap and probably for nothing sometimes.

Philippe's make their own mustard with warning labels on them "BEWARE" No just kidding but it is very hot, and just a taste will do you. It makes your noise run, but there is something about it that makes you dip for more.

There is every kind of salad, desert and cheap coffee. Coffee was five cents a cup until 1977 and it doubled in price to ten cents a cup and now it is forty-five cents.

After stuffing yourself, upon leaving you bump into an old-fashion candy counter that also sells newspapers, cigarettes and chewing gum. (Philippe's. Com)

After all that, we dropped by Ted's Mother's right across the street from Echo Park. I asked if Ann and I could walk over to the park and the answer was, "No".

We were back home by 8:00 p.m. with wonderful memories tucked in my head that have lasted forever and always to remember.

Ann and I did not deserve such a wonderful day. I deserved a switching and even more. However, being treated so well made us both feel guilty and ashamed of our self.

Which in a way was a terrible punishment. A switching would have just been forgotten with time. My mother would have killed me if she had found out about our bus adventure trying to find Olvera Street.

Ann and I had many experiences together, enough to write a book. We stayed best friends through tenth grade.

Ted and Julian bought a new tract home in Norwalk CA at the end of my tenth year. I was happy to leave the coop because it was such an embarrassment. It was a real dump, but my mother was a very good homemaker and even in that dump she keep it spotless, and tried to decorate it.

I had no right to be embarrassed I had become prideful and was jealous of pretty homes. I did not want to leave my "Arkie" family but things were changing, some of my friends had moved away, we were in high school now, our childhood was over and I was glad.

ALL SWEPT UNDER THE RUG

One day after we moved, we were all sitting at the table and the doorbell rang. Moms said, "Go answer it, Peggy. And I opened the door to find Ann standing there with her whole family.

Mom knew they were on their way and wanted to surprise me. They bought a house in Whittier and Ann and I would be attending Whittier High School together. We were inseparable best friends. We graduated from Whittier High in 1953.

We both married sailor boys, and moved to San Diego. Our first babies were just a couple of months apart. She had a baby girl and I had a baby boy.

The world's thorny switch took up residence in Ann's home. Shortly after her baby was born she received some hard slashes, welts and wounds from the world's thorny switch.

Ann was married five times and had one girl and three boys. Two divorces and three husbands died of cancer. Her first marriage ended because both had an affair started at a neighborhood party. Her second husband died of cancer. Her third husband beat her and she divorced him. The last two died of cancer.

We lost contact in 2004 but the last time I talked to Ann she was telling me that she had a friend in Jesus, so I know that soon we will continue where we left off and the worlds thorny switch will never again come to hurt, rob and steal.

CHAPTER THIRTY-ONE

Some say all is forgiven but never forgotten. God says all is forgiven and forgotten no matter how rotten. What about shame that can't be explained? Sweep that shame under the rug unless you accept the fall with a shrug. You can't see the shame under the under the rug but we know that it is there because it grows with despair. It needs to come out for air.

When I was a child I never shared my burden with my friends. I never told anyone but my mother. My mother did the telling to her family and friends. I swept it all under the rug. I pretended a happy family, and respectively referred to Ted as daddy. The older I got the less Ted bothered me and it made it easier. But when Ted came after me I would tell my mother, and all hell would break out.

Ted would convince her that I was just trying to cause trouble because he didn't give me something I wanted. And I was nothing but a spoiled brat.

Our family would go through a period of depression because of me telling on Ted. I would wish that I hadn't told and each time I promised my self that I would never tell again. But I always did and it caused so much trouble. But soon it would be all swept under the rug.

I had some wonderful friends and they became my diversion from an unhappy situation. My baby brother was my solace and I got to take care of him for a long time.

When Teddy Glenn became older he resented any baby sitter especially his sister telling him what to do. By the time Teddy Glenn was seven he no longer wanted me baby sitting him and we were less affectionate toward each other. I thought Ted and Mom spoiled him rotten and Teddy Glenn thought I was a mean sister.

I went to work at F.W. Woolworth at age fifteen for seventy-five cents an hour. I soon was promoted to eighty cents an hour. I loved working for Woolworth. I had so much experience working in the concession stands that I did quite well. Mr. Firman my boss really liked me and encouraged me to become a buyer for the company. I worked Wednesday and Friday's after school from 5:00 p.m. until 900:p.m. I worked on Saturday from 9:00 a.m. until 5:00 p.m.

I always wanted to have a two-wheel bike and could ride one when I was four years old. Ted said, "No! They are too dangerous." I was fourteen before I got a two-wheel bike of my own. Ted would not buy Teddy Glenn a two-wheel bike either. He didn't care if someone else bought him one. Ted did not want the responsibility that he was the one that bought a two-wheeler for Teddy Glenn if he should have an accident and be hurt.

The buyers from F.W. Woolworth brought beautiful bikes into the store to be sold for Christmas. I asked Mr. Firman, my boss, "If I could put one on lay-away for my brother for Christmas." He was eight or nine years old. He didn't have a bike and I wanted him to have one. It left me without any money for a while because I had to pay mom a percentage out of my earnings for room and board and buy my own shoes and clothes now that I was working,

My life was good. All my friends were special to me. My friends and I double dated in high school. We went to all the high school rallies and games. Saturday night we danced at the Hollywood Palladium with the Big Bands. Soon we were dancing at the Hollywood Palladium with Lawrence Welk and his champagne music. Sunday's we were at the beach.

I was married at seventeen and yes there were consequences but we struggled through them and will be married sixty-five years this coming February. We both graduated from high school but that was not enough education to accomplish our dreams. My husband would have been drafted in the army for the Korean conflict if he had not joined the Navy when he did.

God blessed us in so many ways in spite of our immaturity, and foolish choices. My uncle Merle helped David, my husband, be hired as an apprentice in the upholstering department with the Railroad. He was then hired at Greyhound bus lines, where he worked until he retired with a pension. Because of his military benefits we were able to buy a home with a very small down payment. We raised our two boys' in that home for twenty-one years.

David was able to continue his education. He received an Associates Degree in electronics. He opened his own business and worked for another twenty years after he retired from Greyhound.

I was nineteen when my first baby boy was born and I was twenty-one when my second baby boy was born. I too achieved a few skills: Community College for business skills, California Cosmetologist license, Real Estate and Property Management License for Oregon and Nevada. And I was a graduate from Global University in Theology.

My best, and my husband's best, blessing from God are our two boys. They are a joy and with God's help we zipped through their teen years with little trouble. We are extremely proud of them both. I could spend a thousand pages just bragging. Best of all is that my boys and their wives and children are "Born Again Christians." We have six Grandchildren and eight Great Grandchildren and hope for more.

The End

REFERENCES

CHAPTER 1
Article: California in World War 11 Los Angeles Metropolitan Area. (www.militarymuseum.org)
Los Angeles County Hospital (Wikipedia)

CHAPTER 7
Civilian Conservation Corps – Facts & Summary – History

CHAPTER 12
WW 11 Window Banners: (Wikipedia encyclopedia)

CHAPTER 13
Gonorrhea – (WebMD) – What can You Catch in Restrooms?

CHAPTER 19
Dust Bowl - Wikipedia
Facts & Summary - History.Com

CHAPTER 26
Japanese Relocation Camps: The Battle of Los Angeles - Weird California.
California Military History World War 11: Internment of the Japanese Americans.
Phantom Japanese Raid on LA During WW11

ABOUT THE AUTHOR:

Beverly jean McCoy (Harlow) is a native of S. California. She is a Graduate of Whittier High 1953, and married in 1953. Obtained a Cosmetology license, Real Estate license in Oregon and Nevada. Graduate from Global University, Bible teacher and Prison ministry. My greatest achievement is being the Mother of two wonderful boys that grew up to be happily married wonderful men.

Lightning Source UK Ltd.
Milton Keynes UK
UKHW020829241122
412742UK00005B/213